Troubled Heart

Troubled Heart

Reed Family Series, Book 2

Tyora Moody

Tymm Publishing LLC
Columbia, SC

Troubled Heart
Reed Family Series, Book 2

Copyright © 2016 by Tyora Moody

Published by Tymm Publishing LLC
701 Gervais Street, Suite 150-185
Columbia, SC 29201
www.tymmpublishing.com

Cover Design: TywebbinCreations.com
Copy Editing/Proofreading: Felicia Murrell

"Peace I leave with you; my peace I give you. I do not give to you as the world gives. Do not let your hearts be troubled and do not be afraid."

— *John 14:27 NIV*

Prologue

Two Years Ago

Toni Reed sensed the next few minutes would not go well for her.

As soon as Paul Lambert's handsome face turned red, she knew. His blond side-swept bangs lay plastered across his forehead. The charmer's usually playful blue eyes gleamed bright with anger. He shouted, "Were you trying to sabotage me?"

"No!" She backed away from Paul's piercing stare bumping into the chair. "No," she yelled, her eyes wide with fright. It felt like the air had been sucked out of the room. *This must be what it feels like to be in the room with a wild animal where any sudden movements could result in a strike.* The crazy thing was Paul had never laid a hand on her before. She tried to convince herself he would calm down and walk away.

I've seen him like this before.

Toni glanced at the wall behind Paul. Less than a month ago, she watched in horror as he punched a hole in the wall above his entertainment system. Books and DVD's crashed to the floor as Paul swept his arm across the top shelf. The hole had since been covered up with one of *her* paintings, all the items neatly put back in place and not a word said about the incident.

Taking a deep breath, she tried to appear calm. "You know I would never do anything to sabotage you. I want you to look good. We talked about this last night. Remember? You said it was an important point."

Paul stepped forward, "I had it under control. You're trying to say you could do it better. That I don't know what I'm doing. You made me look like an idiot."

That's not how I remember it. Why is he blowing this out of proportion?

Her heart pounded when she saw Paul's clenched fists. Toni shook her head. "No, no...I just wanted to make sure you told him the benefits you could bring to his company."

"You wanted me to appear like I was desperate and didn't know my own company. He will never invest now."

"That's not true. You did a great job and —" Before she could finish her sentence, Paul grabbed her by the shoulders and pushed her against the wall. She cried out in pain as her head bounced off the hard surface.

"You ruined everything! I saw the look on his face."

The back of her head throbbed as she tried to focus. She wheezed, "What is wrong with you?"

Paul's hand came across her face.

He's crazy!

Anger surged. She was no match for Paul's size, but she had to get away from him. Lifting her right knee, she shoved it up as high as she could into his groin area.

Paul groaned from the impact and loosened his grip on her arm. "You — "

Toni wrenched her arm away and wasted no time moving around him. She had to get out of there. Her bag was on the coffee table. She grabbed it and moved quickly to the front door. As soon as she reached it, she felt a strong hand grab her shoulder.

She screamed and turned, swinging her heavy bag across Paul's face.

He stumbled from the blow, but it didn't prevent him from reaching. He wrapped his arms around her body. Toni felt her feet lift off the carpet. She struggled and screamed. Suddenly her body was thrown across the room, crashing into the coffee table.

She cried out in pain as she felt something snap in her arm.

Through her tears, she saw Paul looming over her.

God, help me!

Chapter 1

Two Years Later, Wednesday, June 7 at 12:45 pm

Do you feel safe?

Toni chewed thoughtfully on her chicken salad sandwich as the question lingered in the air awaiting her response. She swallowed, lifting her napkin to her face slowly to wipe her mouth. The answer should've been a simple yes or no, but her mind was flooded with confusing thoughts.

She sensed her older sisters, Asia and Jo, anticipating her answer. It was Jo's turn to make their weekly lunch, so they were assembled around her kitchen table for their get together. If their mother were here, Toni would not have the luxury of time to thoughtfully give an answer. Her mother's stare would have demanded a quick response despite the fact Toni was twenty-seven years old. Thankfully, their mom was hundreds of miles away enjoying a much needed vacation.

Toni knew her sisters were trying their best to be supportive without being pushy. Everyone seemed to be more protective lately, bringing their motherly instincts to the surface. Only ten minutes younger than her twin brother, she understood the protectiveness came with the territory of being the baby of the family. It also didn't help that the *anniversary* of her assault was just around the corner.

Toni adjusted her glasses and attempted to smile. "It's been almost two years. No worries. I'm sure he's moved on. I certainly have."

Sort of. Sure, she'd moved on in many areas of her life, but she still wasn't interested in dating.

Asia, the oldest of the Reed clan, shook her head back and forth slowly making her long ponytail swing like a horse's tail. She never held back her opinions. "That's because he had no choice. The judge filed a no contact protective order against him." Folding her arms, she took on a same similar stance she used in the courtroom when questioning a witness. "Seriously, do you really want Paul Lambert to have access to you again?"

Jo, who was in her first trimester, rubbed her

pregnant belly. "We're not trying to gang up on you, sis, but Asia is right. You need to give this some thought."

"Because if you don't renew this protective order, it's going to be hard for a judge to issue another one," Asia warned.

Toni loved her sisters and knew they meant well. "I know, I know. I'll give it some thought, but I doubt I will ever run into Paul Lambert again. With his good looks and charmed life, I'm sure he's not thinking about me."

Jo smiled, "If he was smart, he would know not to come up against the Reed family again."

They all laughed. The Reed family was known as a crime fighting family. Despite being on a leave of absence, Jo was a homicide detective. Asia worked for the district attorney. Toni's twin brother, Cori worked as a crime scene investigator. To top it all off, their dad was the former chief of police for the Charlotte Mecklenburg Police Department.

It wasn't until after Paul assaulted her that Toni found out he was bipolar. She just knew on occasion he appeared to be on an energetic high, working long hours a day on his startup company. She assumed his irritability and angry outbursts were the result of stress. She learned the hard way that Paul had purposely stopped taking his meds on the notion that he didn't need them anymore.

Her family insisted she file charges. From the very beginning, neither her parents nor her siblings liked Paul. Toni was blindly convinced, in her love-infatuated state, that maybe her family didn't appreciate her dating a white man. Even now, she wanted to kick herself for being so naive. Her mother had warned her there was something lurking under Paul's surface. Everyone could see it, except Toni. Only after landing in the hospital with a bruised face, cracked ribs and a broken arm did Toni finally see the light.

Paul was like no other man she'd ever been with, not that she had been with many men. She could count on one hand the number of boyfriends she'd ever had. Paul was the son of the Lambert family, a descendant of old Southern money. Determined to make his own way, Paul was actively recruiting investors for his startup during the time he dated Toni. She never found out if that one investor Paul wanted desperately on board came through after that night. More than likely, if Paul lost the investor it was due to her assault getting picked up by the local media.

Still, Paul didn't serve a day in prison. He got off

with court ordered rehabilitation and a protective order to have no communication or contact with her. Though she hadn't heard from him, her six months with Paul had left a lasting impression. She often wondered if he'd stayed consistent with his medication or if he had hurt anyone else.

Toni rubbed her left arm. Thankfully, she was right-handed. If she had been unable to do her work, she would've slipped into a deeper depression. Still being able to paint was her therapy.

Jo stood up, clearing dishes off the table.

Asia watched Jo. "How are you doing, Jo? I know you have to be itching to get back to work by now."

Jo placed the dishes on the counter and opened the dishwasher. She looked up. "I have my days. Right now, I'm just happy to finally be over this morning sickness."

Asia shook her head. "I don't see how you do it. I would be crazed right about now."

Toni was grateful the conversation had shifted away from her to Jo's life. Jo decided to take a leave of absence after a difficult homicide case last fall. The timing was perfect to work on her crumbling marriage with her husband, Bryan. From what Toni could see, her nephew B.J. had blossomed having his mother at home with him and was looking forward to becoming a big brother.

Toni's iPhone rang in her bag. She reached inside, pulled it out and peered at the screen. For a second, she froze.

Why is he calling me?

She got up from the table and walked towards the French doors that led out to Jo's patio. She answered on the third ring, "Hello?"

"Hi, Toni. It's Cam. It's been awhile."

Toni couldn't stop the smile that spread across her face. She'd recognize his deep voice anywhere. Detective Cameron Noble was her brother's best friend. They'd known one another since they were kids. "It's been a few months." *Not that I'm keeping track.* "Is this an official call?"

Cam cleared his throat. "I need your assistance on a case. I saw the great work you did for Jo last year on her case. Your composite really helped them find that guy."

After her assault, Toni had taken a forensic art course at her dad's suggestion. A little hesitant about it at first, she soon realized she'd found her niche alongside her siblings. Composites weren't always easy to sketch, but she had a few successes that resulted in arrests and eventual convictions. "Sure, when do you need me?"

"This case is time-sensitive. I have a woman who was assaulted last night, possible concussion. She refused the doctor's recommendations and left the hospital instead of staying the night. I convinced her we could help her since she saw her attacker's face."

Toni turned to see Asia and Jo watching her through the French doors. She smiled and waved. They both turned away. The irony of their conversation a few minutes ago about her own assault fell on Toni. Momma always told her God would work out what happened to her so she could help someone else. Maybe this was her chance.

"I can be at the station in thirty minutes, depending on lunch hour traffic."

"Thanks, Toni. I'll see you soon."

She walked back inside the kitchen to find questioning looks on her sisters' faces.

Jo asked, "Everything okay?"

Toni nodded. "That was Cam. Or, I should say Detective Noble. A woman was assaulted last night. They need a composite of her assailant."

Asia waved her hands in the air. "Ooh, how nice. If I wasn't ten years older, I definitely wouldn't mind being in Detective Noble's presence on a more casual basis." She winked. "Cam grew up to be a nice looking brother."

Toni grimaced. "Who happens to be Cori's best friend."

Asia pursed her lips. "And... Look, one of us needs to be settling down with a nice man. I'm about to hit forty wide open. You, little sis, are still in your twenties. Don't waste time."

Jo shook her head. "Don't pay any attention to her. Her biological clock is a ticking time bomb. You take your time." Jo arched her eyebrow. "This composite Cam asked you to do, isn't this going to be new for you?"

Toni picked up her bag off the table and swung it over her shoulders. "Yeah, I can handle it. Look, I got to go so I can make my way through this traffic. Thanks for lunch, sis."

She reached down and hugged Jo and walked over to hug Asia. She kind of wished their mother was there today too. Toni could've used a Vanessa Reed specialty hug. There was nothing quite like a mama bear hug when she was moving outside her comfort zone.

Up until now, she'd only done a composite

sketch with witnesses not with a victim. She knew a thing or two about wanting justice.

Can I deliver the results this woman needs?

Chapter 2

Wednesday, June 7 at 2:27 pm

Before Toni climbed out of her car, she looked in the rearview mirror. She left Jo's house so fast, she hadn't taken the time to assess her appearance. Her curls had not been affected by the humidity too much. Usually she wore her hair up, but today she opted to let her hair hang down her shoulders. Toni wasn't much for makeup, but she needed something on her lips so she applied a tinted lip gloss she kept in her bag. Finally, she pulled her glasses off and wiped off the smears.

It had been awhile since seeing Cam in person. She grew up with him like he was a brother so she wasn't sure why she was fussing about her appearance. Sure, at one time she was crushing on him, but that was so long ago. He was never interested in her anyway. She was her brother's artsy twin sister. Toni shook her head as if to clear her runaway thoughts.

Girl, let's go!

She reached in the backseat of her red Toyota Rav4 and grabbed her backpack. Toni always kept a notebook and a sketchpad in the bag in case inspiration struck. Unfortunately, today's sketching had nothing to do with her usual art. As she walked towards the building, Toni tried to place herself in the woman's shoes she was about to meet. She remembered the pain and embarrassment she felt when her family came to see her in the hospital. They kept telling her it wasn't her fault, but the entire time she questioned what went wrong.

Sometimes she still reviewed that night over and over in her head. She had sat and watched Paul present the proposed app to the investor. She sensed something was off with Paul. Despite his talkativeness, she'd noticed he wasn't focused, often going off topic. She assumed his behavior was related to being nervous. After hearing him go on and on about the pitch for weeks, she practically knew it herself. Being her overly helpful self, Toni tactfully tried to highlight Paul's main points.

She was haunted by the fact that maybe she should have never tried to help.

Toni cleared her throat. That was the past. It was time to focus.

Drawing a composite sketch was not easy with witnesses who often didn't remember as much detail as they thought. She would have to use her training to carefully ask the victim questions that were going to be uncomfortable for both of them.

She welcomed the blast of cool air as she entered the police department. For a while, she was nervous that somehow she received preferential treatment because her dad was the former chief of police. She did consider it a privilege, but was also happy that she'd proven her skills to be useful a few times as well.

Toni rounded a corner and saw Cam talking on the phone at his desk. He looked up as she approached, winking to acknowledge her presence.

Her heart fluttered a bit. She didn't know if it was her nervousness about seeing the victim or the way Cam winked and flashed his smile at her. She might have thought she'd outgrown her schoolgirl crush, but Asia was right. There was no denying

Cam had grown up to be a chocolate masterpiece. Toni blew out a breath to calm her nerves. As she approached, Cam hung up the phone.

Cam stood, but his smile faded. "Are you okay?"

She hated how her face always betrayed her emotions. Toni nodded. "Yeah, sure. It's been a couple of months since I did a sketch, you know."

"I don't want to push you. Cori said this might not be a good idea."

If her brother were standing there right now, she would've punched him in the shoulder. They might be twins, but that didn't mean he knew her *that* well. "Did he?"

Cam shifted his feet and looked away. "Well, I know what happened to you a few years ago."

"I'm here to help. What's her name?"

Cam eyed her for a few seconds. "Ms. Lewis. Jade Lewis."

Toni shifted her bag to her other shoulder. "Tell me what happened."

"She was on her way home from an event last night. She thought she was the only person in the building. Assailant attacked her from behind. There was just enough light for her to see his face as he was making his exit."

"That's a blessing she saw his face. I'll make sure she feels at ease with me first."

Cam flashed his smile again. "I know you'll do fine, Toni. You have a way about you that I'm sure she will appreciate."

Her face flushed from Cam's comments. Mumbling, "Thanks," she headed around the corner towards the room where she often did her sketches. She knocked on the door and opened it.

When Toni entered, she saw a small, petite woman with her head on the table. Her brown hair was pulled away from her face. As Toni approached, the woman turned slowly to face her. Toni pushed her glasses up on her nose. Jade Lewis was probably a pretty woman, but at the moment, the right side of her face was a mixture of black and blue bruises. Toni observed the woman watching her. Her eyes were dull at first, but something flickered in her eyes.

She's angry. Toni hoped the woman's anger could be channeled to reveal the face of her assailant. It was critical to Toni that she help Jade find the person who did this to her. She held out her hand, "Hello, I'm Toni Reed. I'm here to help you identify your attacker."

Jade shook Toni's outstretched hand. She eyed

the bag where Toni had her sketchpad. "So, I have to tell you the same things I told the detective?"

Toni pulled out the chair across from Jade. "I'm afraid so. Are you ready to get started?"

Jade rubbed her arms as if she were cold. She observed Toni taking out her sketchpad and drawing pencil. Lately, Toni had been trying out a drawing app on her iPad, but she still preferred good old-fashioned pen and paper.

She knew she needed a different approach today and said a silent prayer. Her teacher, the now retired forensic artist, Bobby Askins, would tell her to make sure the victim was comfortable talking. She prayed for God to not only put Jade at ease, but herself as well.

"Jade, what do you do for a living?"

She seemed surprised by the question. "I work as a social media manager at a nonprofit foundation."

"That must be exciting. Which social media do you find you use the most?"

"Facebook and Instagram. I take a lot of photos behind the scene that helps draw attention to the fundraiser."

Toni nodded. "What type of issues or causes does the foundation financially support?"

Jade took a breath. Her shoulders relaxed as she

talked. "The Niles Foundation supports a lot of causes for women. Our main cause is raising money for breast cancer awareness and research."

That was Toni's first cue to glide the interview along. "Was that the purpose of the fundraiser last night?"

She nodded. "Yes. We've been working really hard to promote the event the past three months."

"I imagine you had to stay late and help wrap-up afterwards."

Jade blew softly. "A few of us stayed behind to help clean. I was still uploading photos to Facebook and Instagram when the others called me to help with the cleanup."

Toni smiled. "I'm sure you're very good at what you do and pay a lot of attention to details."

Jade stared off into space. "Yeah, but I forgot my phone in the office, so I had to go back to get it. It was so quiet with no one else there. I thought I was alone, but then I heard a noise. I looked around and started freaking out because I was seeing shadows move or at least that's what I thought."

Jade's fear was so palpable Toni felt the hairs on her arm stand up. "I hurried to the office so I could get my phone and get out of there. As I walked closer to the door, I thought I saw movement ahead of me, which was weird because I thought I heard someone behind me too. I called out, but no one answered. I just kept walking thinking my imagination was running wild from being tired."

Jade raised both hands to her head and rubbed her temples as if to remove the memory from her mind. "As soon as I put my hands on the office doorknob, I felt someone behind me. I turned and something slammed hard against my face. I remember seeing nothing but stars. I felt an arm around my neck and tried to scream. But, he tightened his grip on my throat and pushed me inside the office. At this point, he was choking me and I was struggling to breathe so I just went limp on purpose hoping he would stop."

Toni's hands shook. She needed to be calm so she guided Jade to the next step. "I'm sorry you have to repeat this again. I understand what you went through."

"Do you?" She accused.

Toni responded, "I was assaulted two years ago. My circumstances may be a bit different. I knew my attacker," she gripped the pencil tight. Toni glanced at her hand and loosened her grip, fearing she would break her pencil in half. "Anyway, believe me, you want to bring this person to justice."

"I want you to get him."

Toni hoped she could help Jade. With it being dark, she wondered how much Jade really saw. "So you said you made your body go limp and he stopped? Did you see his face?"

"Yes. He let me go and I just slid to the floor. I kept my eyes closed." Jade touched her throat. "But I opened them just as he walked out. He turned to look back and that's when I saw his face."

Toni wondered about the angle and the lighting. "You got a clear look at his features from the front?"

Jade nodded.

"Do you think you can describe his general features? His race, approximate age, eye color...any minute detail you can remember will be helpful to me."

"He was white. He looked like he could be in his late twenties or early thirties."

"That's good. What about the shape of his face?"

"He had a square jaw."

Toni let her pencil glide across the sketchpad as she quickly outlined the shape of the face.

Jade continued talking, "I remember his eyes. They were blue...and cold. Icy almost, like he didn't care."

"Describe his eyes a bit more. Were they set wide or close together?"

"Close together. He had high cheek bones."

Toni quickly added the eyes and proceeded to fill in the cheekbone structure. She'd seen and studied many faces over the past year. "What else do you remember about him? What about his nose?"

"Long, slim."

"His mouth?"

"Thin lips."

Toni's pencil scratched across the pad. A face was starting to form, but at this point Toni needed confirmation. She flipped the sketchpad around on the table so Jade could view what she'd captured. "Here is what I have so far. We can keep working on the sketch."

Jade studied the composite. She shook her head. "No. His eyes aren't right."

"Okay, that's fine. What are we missing?"

Jade stared. "His eyes should be more narrow. And, his jaw was more square."

Toni was surprised by how much detail the woman was able to remember. She erased portions of her sketch and made the changes Jade suggested. The more the face changed, the more Toni started to feel perplexed.

This face seemed familiar.

Toni flipped the sketchpad around and watched Jade's face. Tears formed in the woman's eyes and she began to shake. "That's him! That's him."

Toni stared at the sketch again and felt her own body beginning to shake. Jade just confirmed the sketch was spot on.

Why does this sketch resemble Paul Lambert?

Chapter 3

Wednesday, June 7 at 4:01 pm

Toni was confused. Had she messed up? She'd followed all her training and listened closely to every suggestion Jade made. The sketch wasn't totally accurate, but these were Paul's features. The man had been on her mind the past week and she was just talking about him with her sisters. *Can this really be him?* She knew Paul could turn violent, but why would he be skulking in the Niles Foundation building.

She remembered his bipolar condition. *If Paul isn't on his meds, he can become extremely impulsive.*

She held Jade's gaze. "You're sure this resembles the man you saw last night?"

Jade nodded furiously. "It's him! I will never forget that face."

Toni tried to be calm. All she was supposed to do was get a composite sketch. She did what she needed to do.

Still she had to ask. "Have you ever seen him before?"

Jade frowned, shaking her head. "I don't think so."

Toni reigned in her thoughts. She didn't want to add any more stress to the victim. "You did good, Jade." Toni tore the page from her pad. She couldn't look at the sketch anymore. "I will give this to Detective Noble. He'll consult with you about what's next in the investigation."

"I hope he catches him."

"Me too."

Toni's hands shook as she opened the door. She wasn't sure what to think. Paul had been on her mind more so than she wanted the past few days. She still felt like she must have unconsciously included his features in the sketch. It wasn't like she hadn't tried to bring Paul to justice. If he assaulted another woman, his supposed rehab didn't do a thing.

But Jade said she didn't know him.

Cam was at his desk. As she drew near to Cam,

she must have appeared distressed because he stood and she could see his look of concern.

"How did it go?"

She passed the sketch to him. "Good. I think."

He took it and examined it. "This is pretty detailed."

"Yeah, she said it was him."

Cam placed the sketch on his desk and held out his hand towards the chair next to his desk. "Why don't you sit for a minute? You did a good job, but you look a bit shaken up to me. Let me talk to Ms. Lewis first."

Toni nodded. Her knees did feel weak. She plopped in the chair, letting her bag slide to the floor. She wasn't sure if she should say what was on her mind or not. She didn't want Cam to think she was losing it. As she pondered the similarities from the sketch, she tried to convince herself it was nothing.

Cam appeared around the corner. He peered at her. "Are you sure you're okay? I know that must have been hard."

Toni swallowed. "It was hard to hear, but I made sure she was comfortable and that she trusted me. There are a few details bugging me though."

Cam sat and slid his chair closer to her. "Okay."

The more Toni thought about it, there were two main things that seemed odd to her.

"First, I was surprised by how much detail she remembered since she said the place was dark."

Cam said, "I thought that as well when I heard her statement, but I went by the building this morning. There's a walkway between the gallery and the office where she was assaulted. It's possible that light from the surrounding buildings and the moonlit sky came through the door at just the right moment. She mentioned she saw his face when he turned towards her."

"She's blessed to be alive. I guess this guy didn't think she would be able to identify him."

Cam folded his arms. "She was smart with letting her body go limp. I suspect this man was there for another reason and he wasn't expecting anyone to be in the building. It's possible someone wanted something out of the gallery. They do keep pretty pricey items inside. Even though the owner claims the gallery was locked tight, I asked for an inventory and for her to let me know if anything was missing. It's possible Ms. Lewis could have been in the way of a robbery."

Toni frowned. *A robbery?* Paul was a wealthy

man, so he certainly didn't need to stick around to steal.

Cam continued, "I'm also going through the guest list for the fundraiser since it had to be someone with an invitation. There were approximately six men in attendance. Most of the attendees were women. This person had access and could have found a way to stick around after everyone left."

Toni shook her head. "Yeah, but why not just stay in the shadows until she left? Why attack Jade?"

Cam shrugged. "That's a good point. Maybe the person panicked. Or they could have wanted to throw off the real reason they were there." He studied her face. "You still look troubled. What else is bothering you?"

She was sure Cam had seen her with Paul a few times. "Look at the sketch. Does this guy look familiar?"

Cam stared at her, picking the sketch up from his desk. He peered intently at the sketch again and shook his head. "No, I don't think so." He looked at her. "Are you saying you know this face?"

"I hope I haven't screwed this up, but this sketch looks a lot like Paul Lambert to me."

"Your ex-boyfriend? The guy who assaulted you?" Cam blew out a breath. "That would be quite the coincidence for you. But he does have a history of violence."

Toni continued, still trying to process her thoughts. "Paul is the kind of guy who does things in the heat of the moment, especially if he stopped taking his meds. It sounds like this person who stayed around was more purposeful. Maybe you're right, this person was waiting in the wings so they could get access to something in the gallery."

Cam held up his hands. "The latter scenario seems more reasonable to me. Keep in mind I have a guest list here. Paul Lambert's name is not on this list."

Toni sighed. "Well, that's good. Look, I'm sorry. I just thought I should tell you. I know how important details are to an investigation. Right before you called, I was talking to my sisters about Paul. The protective order expires soon and I'm not sure if it needs to be renewed."

Cam narrowed his eyes. "Maybe you should get it renewed. That's probably what's bothering you after seeing Ms. Lewis."

"You could be right. Still, would you mind keeping me updated?"

"Sure thing, but I don't want you worried about this. You did your part with the sketch. Besides, all of us supposedly have a person in the world who look exactly like us."

"A doppleganger." Toni stated.

"Yeah...that." Cam grinned.

Toni stood. "But you will check to see if Jade has any connection to Paul, right?"

Cam's smile disappeared. "If that will give you some peace of mind, sure." He slid his chair back and stood. "I need to talk to the captain about releasing the sketch to the media. Whoever this guy is, we'll find him."

"All right. I appreciate you calling me in."

"Thank you for lending us your talents."

As she turned to walk away, what Cam really said sunk in. It would be better for someone else to ID the sketch as Paul Lambert if that was the case. Of course, he'd also just said Paul was not on the guest list.

So, why am I still stressing over the sketch?

As Toni exited the building, she wondered if she'd just made a complete fool of herself in front of Cam. She basically let it be known that she still had issues. Of course, as much as Cam and her brother hung out, it wasn't a secret that she'd stayed to herself after the assault.

After she climbed inside her car, Toni sat for a few minutes with the air condition on full blast. She didn't consider herself the investigative person in the family. That was more her siblings' territory. She knew she needed to let Cam deal with his investigation, but as she drove off, questions continued to hound her.

Is there any connection between Paul and Jade? What could have been so valuable that it resulted in a woman's assault?

Chapter 4

Wednesday, June 7 at 6:08 pm

When Toni arrived home, she wasn't sure what to do first. Full of questions, she wanted to talk to someone. She certainly didn't want to approach either one of her sisters, especially after their lunchtime conversation. Both of her older sisters could make a situation more dramatic than necessary. Toni often sought out her mother first because she felt like she really listened. While Vanessa Reed's advice was not always appreciated, all of her children agreed Mama Bear was the one they went to for support. Their parents, Justice and Vanessa Reed, were on a ten day cruise in the Caribbean. All of the siblings, including their half-brother Jax, had chipped in to send their parents on the cruise.

Toni thought out loud, "It would be unfair for me to call. The ship left the Charleston port on Monday. They'll return next week. That sketch could be anyone." She knew she should listen to Cam and wait to see what happens when the sketch went public.

For some reason, that wasn't good enough for her. Toni dialed her brother's number. If anyone would set her straight, Cori would. Out of all her siblings, Cori had the same calming presence their mother had.

Cori answered on the second ring. "What's up, Sis?"

"Are you busy?"

"Naw. I'm about to order some food. You want to come over?"

"I'm starving. I'll be there shortly."

It didn't take long for Toni to drive to her brother's apartment. They lived approximately ten minutes from each other. That's why she stayed in Charlotte. She liked being able to drop in to see her parents or hang out with her siblings. She loved her big Southern city with its hometown feel.

She knocked on Cori's door and he opened it with a big grin. His smile wavered as he eyed her. "Uh-oh, something's up."

"Sorry, Bro. You're the only one I can talk to right now." She brushed past Cori and entered his apartment. Surprisingly, for a bachelor, Cori kept his place neat and orderly. Being a crime scene investigator, Cori was detailed and logical about most everything in his life. Her brother was also the nerd of the family, while she tended to be the artistic one. Where her apartment walls were covered with her own art, Cori's walls resembled a sophisticated adolescent. Posters of several science fiction films like Star Wars and Matrix were framed. Toni had helped him find the frames.

She followed her brother through his living room towards his kitchen. Two large pizzas lay on the table.

Toni reached for a paper plate. "Were you planning a party?"

Cori flipped open the first pizza and grabbed a slice of pepperoni. "No, but I should warn you Cam said he might drop by."

Toni held her hand with the plate in mid-air. "You could have told me he was coming over."

Cori chewed the pizza. "You said you needed to talk. Besides, he won't be here for another hour. He may not make it at all. This is the third time in a few weeks we've been trying to get together."

"Oh, I see. Speaking of Cam, why are you talking about me with him?"

Cori grinned. "I take it he asked you to help him with his current case? Good for you to work together."

"What's that supposed to mean?"

Toni hated when her brother had that knowing look like he knew her so well. She pointed her finger at him. "I told you about playing matchmaker."

He shrugged. "Cam's a good guy. He certainly has a track record that's better than some other guys from your past."

Toni couldn't argue with him on that one, but for the millionth time she wasn't interested in dating and she certainly didn't want to be in a relationship with Cam Noble.

"Hey, what time is it?" She jumped up and grabbed the remote from Cori's coffee table. Maybe she would catch the end of the six o'clock news.

Cori asked, "You looking for the sketch on the news? I'm sure you did a good job."

Toni really wanted someone else to look at the sketch and tell her she wasn't crazy. She sat back down so she could face the television. "This was a different experience today. The face looked familiar to me. I almost thought maybe I unconsciously added features."

Cori wiped his hands with a paper towel. "You were trained to learn common facial features."

"I know. The victim was detailed about her description despite the fact her surroundings were dark."

Cori nodded. "The mind is pretty incredible. It can retain more detail from a traumatic experience than we realize."

A memory flashed in Toni's mind. She could still see Paul's face contorted in rage as he stood above her. That image often haunted her in her sleep. She shook away the memory and gazed at the television. The NBC *Nightly News* with Les Holt was on instead of the local news. She pulled her iPhone out of her bag and clicked Safari to find her bookmark for the Charlotte-Mecklenburg Police Department.

There it was. It was always amazing to see her composite sketches posted for the world to see.

She passed her phone to Cori. "Take a look. Does that look like anyone you know?"

Cori stared at the image on her phone. "I don't know. Nobody comes to mind."

Toni didn't know whether to be relieved or

exasperated. Cori had spent more time around her and Paul than her other siblings.

He asked, "Who does it remind you of?"

She bit her lip. "Paul."

Cori's eyes opened wide. "What?" For a minute, he studied the image on the phone again. "I mean, I guess there is some resemblance."

"Or he was just on my mind. I told Cam I thought the sketch looked like Paul."

Cori raised his eyebrow. "Why?"

Toni waved her hands. "I've been around Asia, Jo and you enough to know unshared details can wreck a case. I just didn't want my composite to be a problem later."

"Calm down, Sis. You've been trained and you're good at what you do. Remember you only sketched what the victim told you and she had to confirm what you sketched, right?"

Toni slumped in the chair. "She said it was him."

"Okay. You know just because the sketch resembles Paul doesn't mean it's him."

"So, I made a fool of myself in front of Cam for no reason."

"I'm sure that's not how he saw it. Cam was just as angry as all of us after what Paul did to you.

I never told you, but both of us confronted Paul while you were in the hospital."

Toni's mouth dropped open.

"Yeah, Cam can be a big intimating guy and believe me... We didn't touch Paul, but I know we scared him."

"I had no idea."

The doorbell rang.

"That's Cam now. Are you staying?"

Toni shook her head. "Uh, I probably should go."

"You didn't eat anything." He lifted the lid on the other pizza box. "I ordered spinach and chicken for you. At least take the box home."

She hadn't eaten since lunch so she wasn't going to refuse her brother. When she was worried, she had a tendency to forget about eating. Toni picked up the box and turned to see Cori open the door. Cam stepped in dressed in a t-shirt and jeans.

Oh my!

Even in casual wear, Cam looked like he stepped out of a fashion magazine.

He grinned at her. "Good to see you twice in one day."

"Yeah. Sorry I can't stay, busy day tomorrow. I'm

just checking in with my brother." She held up the pizza box. "Oh, and getting a free meal too."

"Next time the meal is on you." Cori pointed at her and walked back towards the kitchen leaving her to face Cam.

"You did good today. Captain gave the approval to release the sketch to the public. You should start seeing it tonight on the eleven o'clock news."

Toni looked at Cam. "Good, I hope someone recognizes him. Jade needs to be able to get justice. She has a difficult time ahead."

"I have every intention of catching this guy."

Toni sensed he wanted to talk more, but she really couldn't stay much longer. "Sorry, I have to go."

"Let me help." Cam reached over and opened the door.

She squeezed by him towards the door feeling like an electric current jolted her. Good thing she had a good grip on the pizza box or she would have dropped it.

Cam followed her as she started walking to her car. She wasn't expecting that, but it was probably a good thing because she wasn't always good with juggling items in her hand. "Can you hold this?"

He reached out and held the pizza box as she dug

for her keys in her bag. Once she retrieved them, she clicked the locks. "I appreciate your help."

He stared at her. "Are you still worried this guy is Paul?"

Am I that obvious? "It's bothering me a little. I'm sure I just made a big deal out of nothing."

"Well, I wanted you to know I'll look into his whereabouts. Discreetly."

She looked at him. "Thanks, Cam. I appreciate it."

Cam waited until she climbed inside the car and started the engine. He waved goodbye and headed inside Cori's apartment.

Toni backed out of the apartment complex feeling a bit calmer than she did when she arrived. She came for her brother's support and drove away with comfort from a source she wasn't expecting.

Chapter 5

Thursday morning, June 8 at 11:32 am

Toni was determined to stay out of Cam's way though she was really curious about any response to the composite. When she watched the eleven o'clock news last night, the anchorman mentioned there was a robbery at the Niles Foundation and that a staff member had been assaulted. Toni wondered what the person had stolen.

To curb her curiosity, she busied herself with her brand new venture, designing jewelry. Unlike her siblings, Toni was a bit more entrepreneurial. She just couldn't hang at a nine-to-five job. She started selling her art as prints and soon moved into creating everything from greeting cards to handcrafted bags. With some business pointers and web design help from her childhood friend,

Angel Cade, she'd launched her online business a year ago. Angel had arrived earlier to help Toni take photos of the latest additions for her store.

Toni turned from her kitchen table, which often served as her workspace more than her eating space. She watched Angel pack her DSLR camera.

Angel grinned, "I uploaded the images to Dropbox for you. You should be able to size them in Photoshop in a few minutes."

Toni clapped her hands. "I can't wait. I've been working on these bracelets and necklaces for three months. I've had some good feedback from my Instagram followers on the earlier pieces."

"I saw. You're going to be sold out once you upload these images to your Etsy store."

"I hope so! I enjoyed working with the various stones. This was a different experience than painting. I needed a change."

Angel nodded. "There's healing and peace that comes from being creative."

Toni watched as Angel waddled over to the couch. "You know, between you and Jo, I feel surrounded by pregnant women."

Angel laughed. "Well I'm due in a few weeks so that will soon change. I can't wait to deliver this baby."

"I guess I'll have my hands full with babysitting requests."

"Good training for when you have your own child one day."

"Sure would be nice to find a husband first." Though Toni hadn't been dating, she still longed for a family.

Angel walked over and hugged Toni. "God knows your desires. In fact, He may have already placed the man for you in your life. That's kind of how it turned out for Wes and me. We knew each other when we were kids. Who knew we would later get married and have a baby boy on the way?"

Toni smiled as Cam's face flashed in her mind.

"Somebody or something is on your mind," Angel commented.

Toni shook her head. "No."

"You know, as I was taking photos this morning, I was thinking these would make great pieces for a wedding party. You should ask Lenora Freeman about placing these in her bridal shop."

Toni tilted her head. "I hadn't thought about that. I need to make you my marketing person too."

"You're doing just fine. I've seen your Instagram following. I got to go. Wes wants to get lunch today before we head to our appointment with our obstetrician."

Toni hugged her friend again. "I'm so happy for you two."

After Angel left, Toni decided to do what she'd been dying to do for two days. She settled onto the couch and grabbed her phone.

Cam answered after the third ring, "Hello?"

His voice warmed her. "Hey Cam, it's Toni."

Cam cleared his throat. "Hey, Toni. Let me guess. You're calling about an update."

Toni suddenly felt like she shouldn't have called. "Is this a bad time?"

"No, no. I just hate to disappoint you. There's been no real leads yet." Cam paused. "I was able to get a handle on Paul Lambert's whereabouts Tuesday evening though."

"You were?" Toni took a deep breath.

"He has an alibi." Cam grew quiet.

She swallowed. For some reason, Toni felt like Cam was leaving something out. "Okay. I'll let you go. It's not like you don't have a ton of cases in front of you."

"Wait, Toni. There is something I found out. I'm not sure if you want to know."

"Is it about Paul?"

"Yeah. Paul has a fiancée. I didn't know if you knew."

Fiancee.

"Are you okay?"

"Yeah. I'm just wondering if this woman knows what she's getting into."

"Well, maybe he's changed. You didn't back down from filing charges."

"He got off easy as far as I'm concerned."

Toni realize she sounded bitter. It wasn't her intentions to go there, but Paul could easily go off his meds again and cause damage during a manic episode.

"Cam, I don't want to take up any more of your time. I do hope you find out who attacked Jade. I hope I haven't interfered in your investigation."

"Not at all. You did your job. The composite will jar someone's mind. Don't worry about it anymore."

"Thanks, Cam." Toni hung up the phone.

She knew Cam was trying to comfort her, but unlike the other night, she was still troubled. Paul had moved on with his life. Despite her growth in other parts of her life like her business and her work with the police, she was still alone. She simply couldn't bring herself to trust another man.

She'd never experienced that kind of rage from someone else before and didn't want to again.

Toni got up from the couch and picked up her iPad off the kitchen table. When her mind went in a negative direction, she tried to busy herself with work. She swiped through the photos Angel had uploaded. After fiddling with one of the photos, she uploaded a sneak peek post of her new collection to her Instagram account.

She remembered Jade mentioning being a social media manager. *What was the name of the organization?*

The Niles Foundation.

She switched over to Safari and searched for the organization on Google. After she selected the search results, she watched as a pretty coral themed website loaded. Toni surfed through the website noting that the foundation was named after a woman named Juliette Niles. The founder was a young woman who appeared to be close to her own age.

Toni didn't see any mention of Jade on the website's staff page, but saw the Instagram icon. When she pulled up the profile page, Toni assumed the photos were from the same place where Jade was attacked.

As she scrolled down the feed, there was a pattern of photos that consisted of scrumptious food and well-dressed people. Her eyes stopped on one photo that was about six weeks old. It was a picture of the founder Olivia Niles. But what really caught Toni's eye was the man next to her.

It was Paul Lambert.

"No way!" Toni blew out a breath.

The more she stared at Paul and the woman in his life, the more it dawned on Toni.

If Jade worked for Olivia Niles, perhaps she knew Paul.

Cam had mentioned Paul had an alibi, but he didn't provide any further information.

Toni prayed the direction her mind was taking her wasn't going to lead down a path she would soon regret.

Chapter 6

Friday, June 9 at 10:32 am

There had been many nights after Paul's brutal attack when Toni couldn't sleep. She woke up Friday morning after one of those types of nights. In the past, she'd stared at the ceiling questioning if she did something wrong, even wondering why God allowed Paul to cross her path. Why was she charmed by him in the first place? She often wondered over the months after Paul's rehabilitation sentence if he would hurt another woman. How diligent was he really about taking his meds now? Was his fiancée even aware of Paul's mental illness?

With those thoughts hounding her most of the night, by morning, Toni had decided she needed to see Jade again. She didn't want to question the woman about the attack, but she did want to learn more about her boss, Olivia Niles. After a shower, Toni armed herself with a cup of coffee and browsed her iPad to find out more about the Niles Foundation. She noticed the address was located downtown Charlotte so she pulled up the route on her iPhone.

Despite it being mid-morning, it still took Toni time to navigate I-77 due to an earlier accident. She'd almost lost her nerve and wanted to turn around twice before she reached her exit. It wasn't like she didn't have plenty of things to do, but when something bothered her, she just couldn't let it go.

Toni found the office building where the Niles Foundation was located. After securing parking in a nearby garage, she sprinted across the street and entered the building. The first thing she noticed was the security desk setup. An older man with white hair smiled and waved. Large monitors hung on the wall. As she walked by, she glimpsed herself walking towards the elevator.

She stopped to read the wall directory near the elevators. The Niles Foundation was located on the third floor. She also noticed the Juliette Niles Gallery was also on the same floor.

Was this where Jade was assaulted?

Toni pressed the up elevator button and crossed her arms. The building's cold air penetrated straight to her bones causing her to shiver in her sundress. She could have blamed her shakiness on the cold, but she still wasn't sure coming unannounced to Jade's workplace was a good idea.

Toni stepped on the elevator and pressed the number three. As the elevator doors closed, she rubbed her goose bumped covered arms. How often had her mother and siblings warned her about her impulsiveness? It wasn't like she didn't try to think her ideas through. She just often ended up overthinking and choosing the wrong path anyway.

God, I just want to do the right thing here. I don't know why this is bothering me so much. I trust you to lead me in the right direction.

When Toni exited the elevator, it took her a moment to comprehend her surroundings. The Niles Foundation gold embossed logo hung on the wall across from the elevator above the receptionist desk. It appeared the foundation took up the entire third floor. Toni noticed the young woman behind the desk staring at her.

Okay, I need to stop looking crazy.

Toni smiled and walked towards the desk. She peeped at the nameplate, which read Annie Myers. Annie appeared to be near Toni's age. Her thick reddish wavy hair was styled in a side French braid. She wore horn-rimmed gold-plated glasses that sat low on her freckled nose. The woman peered over the frames and flashed a cautious smile, "May I help you?"

"Yes, I met your social media manager the other day. She was telling me about your foundation. I was wondering how I could get involved."

Annie reached for a brochure on the side of her desk. "Would you like to volunteer?"

Toni took the brochure from Annie's outstretched hand. "Volunteering would be great, but I noticed you featured local artists. What's your process for accepting art for your fundraising events?"

"Oh, you probably want to talk to Olivia. She's always looking to work with local artists." Annie frowned, "Who did you say you talked to?"

Toni's heart leapt. She didn't think about having a chance to talk to Olivia directly. "Um, Jade? Jade Lewis."

"Jade?" The young woman's eyes questioned.

Before Toni could respond, a door opened off

from the right of the receptionist area. A group of people swarmed outside of what appeared to be a conference room. One of those people looked very familiar. Toni had studied her Instagram profile several times last night.

The woman walked out of the conference room and approached the receptionist desk. Her long, black hair was slung across her shoulders. It was hard to determine Olivia's background. She had exotic facial features influenced by an Asian heritage.

She briefly glanced in Toni's direction. "Annie, do you have any messages for me? Mr. Stewart was going to call me on my cell phone."

"Nope. No calls." The receptionist glanced at me. "I do have a local artist who's interested in the foundation." She smiled at me. "Sorry, I didn't catch your name."

For a split second, Toni was unsure about sharing her name. This was going way too fast and in a direction she hadn't anticipated. She turned to the woman who was engaged to Paul and held out her hand. "Toni Reed."

Olivia hesitated for a moment.

Toni observed Olivia. *Does she know who I am? Has Paul ever mentioned me?*

Olivia held out her hand, "Toni, it's always a pleasure to meet local artists. I'm Olivia Niles. Are you familiar with our foundation?"

Good thing Toni had done her research so she could pitch her idea to Jade to take to her boss. Now it looked like Toni would have to pull together her elevator pitch herself. She exchanged a handshake with Olivia. "Yes, I know you deal with women's issues. Would you be interested in some pieces that highlight domestic violence or abuse?"

Olivia placed her hands on her chest. "Oh my. You know, we haven't planned an event quite like that yet. We focus mainly on bringing awareness and funding research for breast cancer and other illnesses like heart disease in women. But I will say with both Breast Cancer Awareness and Domestic Violence Awareness being in the month of October, I have thought many times that we should do something. It's just so hard to pull these events together."

"I can imagine. Well, if you're interested, my collection is about healing so it's possible the pieces could work for any of your causes. They're a series of seven watercolor paintings."

"I'm intrigued. I would love to see your

collection." Olivia turned to Annie. "If you do get that call I'm looking for can you forward it to my cell phone? I would like to show Ms. Reed the gallery."

Annie's eyes opened wide, but she seemed to think about how her face must have looked. She blinked and said, "Do you think that's a good idea right now?"

Olivia stared back at Annie. "It's what I always do. No need to stop the routine." Turning back towards Toni, Olivia said, "Why don't you walk with me for a minute? I'd love to show you our gallery. It's a source of pride for me."

Toni caught Annie's face, which appeared too pale. "I appreciate your time, Ms. Niles, but I can come back another time."

"Oh, no. I insist. And please, call me Olivia or better yet, Liv. Besides, I haven't been inside the gallery in a few days. I usually visit at least once a day."

As Toni walked behind Olivia, she observed the woman's sophistication. She glided down the hall like a beauty queen. Really, Olivia and Paul were a beautiful couple.

Olivia turned and smiled. "My mother spent her life as an artist. Our foundation was established for her. I like to visit our gallery because I keep some of her artwork here. It's a way for me to be close to my mother even though she's not physically here anymore."

As they approached the gallery, Toni noticed there was a door on the right roped off with yellow police tape.

Was this where Jade was attacked?

Toni pointed. "Did something happen here?"

Olivia's face appeared flushed. "There was an incident here after our fundraiser the other night."

An incident.

Toni inquired. "I thought I saw something on the news the other night. There was a person of interest sketch."

Olivia eyed Toni for a moment. "Yes, there was someone here that shouldn't have been here. That person managed to get into my gallery too. We're leaving it to the police to figure out what really happened."

Toni frowned.

There was a robbery.

She wanted to ask more questions, but realized she was already in a precarious situation by coming this far.

What would Cam think of her being here?

Chapter 7

She followed Olivia into a breezeway. The sun felt warm against her chilled skin as they walked towards the gallery entrance. Toni looked behind her recalling the details of Jade's story during their session. Toni agreed with Cam's observation. With enough light Jade could have seen her attacker's face.

Olivia punched numbers on a keypad by the door. A click echoed into the hallway indicating the doors were unlocked. When she pushed the double doors open, Toni caught her breath. As she stepped onto the hardwood floors, her eyes fixated on a sculpture more than six feet in height. The piece depicted a woman holding a baby.

Olivia raised her arms. "Isn't this stunning? This

was one of the last pieces my mom did before the cancer took her. It was a massive undertaking for her. Took her three years to complete."

Toni stared. "It's beautiful. Now that I look at it, the foundation's logo has the shape of the sculpture etched in the middle."

Olivia beamed. "Yes! You are an artist. Many people never recognize that."

"So this gallery is used for fundraisers. Is it open to the public?"

"The gallery was built two years ago as a labor of love. We hold two fundraisers a year here. And yes, we open it to the public on Wednesday, Saturday and Sunday afternoons." Olivia's smile faded. "Unfortunately after this week, we may need to keep it closed to the public for a few weeks."

Toni looked around and her eyes fell on a painting on the wall to her right. "I recognize this artist."

Olivia nodded. "Yes, Gloria Anderson. She painted that portrait of the pink roses for the fundraiser we had Tuesday. We sold it. "

Even though she came today for one purpose, Toni thought it would be nice to have her artwork featured here. She'd worked with galleries in the past, but the commission didn't make it easy to sell her paintings. Establishing her own business had been the best move for her.

As they continued walking Toni noticed there was a bare area on the wall. There were marks on the wall indicating the size of the painting.

Where was the painting? Was this the stolen painting?

Toni bent to read the white card that remained. The missing painting, titled *Rose Garden*, was also a Gloria Anderson original. It was painted in 1996. *Twenty years old. Wow. Probably worth a lot of money.*

Behind her she heard someone clear their throat.

Toni stepped back to find Olivia watching her. She waited to see if Olivia would offer any information about the missing painting.

Olivia smiled faintly. "So when can I see your pieces?"

Toni took a deep breath. "You are so kind. I really just came here by chance to see if I could get involved. I can bring my portfolio next week if that's okay."

"Sure, setup a time with Annie at the front desk. I look forward to seeing your work."

"Sounds like a plan."

Olivia narrowed her eyes. "I am curious though.

You mentioned an idea centered on domestic violence. Is this personal?"

Toni swallowed. The thought occurred again that Liv might already know who she was. If so, why wouldn't she come right out and say something? "The collection is pretty personal. In fact, I haven't shown anyone these pieces before, so you would be one of the first to see them."

"Oh, well, I really can't wait." Olivia looked at her phone. "I have a lunch meeting I need to get to in twenty minutes. It was nice of you to stop by. Please feel free to check out the rest of the gallery. The doors will automatically lock behind you."

"Thank you." Toni watched as Olivia walked out. This was not a part of her plan, but she was willing to go with the scenario. If Cam knew what she was doing, he probably wouldn't be too pleased with her.

She walked around the gallery, looking at the various artists. Towards the center of the gallery, a platform and chairs were set up. Toni recognized the set up from the photos she saw on the foundation's Instagram page. With the various paintings and items in the gallery, there had to be a lot more security. She returned her gaze to the wall with the missing painting. She knew that Gloria

Anderson painting had to be worth thousands of dollars. *How did someone break in? They would've had to obtain the security code to enter.*

Toni looked up and noticed several cameras. She wondered how many other places on the floor had cameras.

She moved towards the exit and walked out into the breezeway. The gallery doors clicked behind her. She tried to pull on the doors. They wouldn't budge.

Toni viewed the Charlotte skyline from the windows. It would've been dark, but the windows would have let in a good bit of light from the sky and the surrounding buildings. Jade said she thought she saw a shadow in front of her. Toni noticed cameras on both sides of the walkway. She didn't want Cam to know she was here, but certainly he had to have access to the camera footage.

After Toni entered the hallway, she stopped in front of the taped door. Jade said she was pulled into the office and assaulted. Olivia had described it as an incident.

Incident... That bothers me.

Cam claimed Paul had an alibi, but he didn't elaborate about Paul's whereabouts in Charlotte.

People were known to lie to protect their loved ones. Suppose Olivia conveniently made Paul's name disappear from the guest list?

She looked up towards the ceiling again noting there wasn't a camera near the office door where Jade was assaulted. Toni hadn't noticed before when she followed Liv to the gallery, but right across from the office door was a stairwell. She opened the door and saw the number three on the wall. She didn't notice a camera on the stairwell. For a moment, she thought about exploring the stairwell some more, but changed her mind. There were a lot of questions on her mind for Cam.

As Toni headed back towards the receptionist desk, she saw another camera. That camera was behind the receptionist desk and faced the elevator doors. She also glimpsed a monitor in the corner of the desk she hadn't noticed.

With a security guard downstairs, there was no doubt about the level of security in the building. Surely the person who attacked Jade had to have been aware of the cameras. How did they get in and out undetected? Maybe they used the stairwell to enter and exit the floor.

Annie called out to her. "All finished with your tour?"

Toni smiled but noticed Annie's smile seemed strained. "Thanks for the introduction. I certainly wasn't expecting to meet Olivia Niles or get a tour, especially after the *incident* on Tuesday."

The faint smile disappeared on Annie's face. "Liv is dedicated to this foundation. Sometimes she doesn't use the best judgment. She was impressed with you though. She mentioned you would want to make an appointment."

Doesn't use the best judgment. That was a curious statement.

Toni pulled out her phone. "When would be a good time? I'm self-employed so I'm pretty flexible."

"Must be nice. Well, her first available appointment next week is Tuesday morning at ten o'clock."

"That works for me. By the way, I was asking earlier about Jade Lewis, your social media manager."

Annie scrunched her nose. "Our social media person is Carol Landers."

Toni froze. "Really? Is she new?"

Annie shook her head. "I've been here two years and Carol was already a part of the team. I think

Liv and Carol have known each other since like college."

Now Toni was puzzled. "Oh. Does Carol have interns or other assistants?"

"Sometimes. Yeah, I guess she does, but she's pretty efficient with managing our social media."

Toni asked, "So you don't know a Jade Lewis at all?"

Annie narrowed her eyes. "She's one of our volunteers. Why are you asking? You're not some reporter, are you?"

"No. No. Jade told me about the Niles Foundation. She was *the one* assaulted here the other night."

Annie narrowed her eyes. "You definitely sound like a reporter. Are you really an artist?"

"Oh, I'm definitely an artist, just naturally curious."

Annie peered at her. "We're sorry about what happened to Jade. I will say nothing like this has ever happened before. The detective thinks she got in the way during the robbery."

Toni tried to process what she heard. "I'm sure the detective will find the culprit." Toni smiled. "I'll see you next week."

Annie quickly smiled. "You have a good day and we'll see you next week."

Toni turned and walked over to press the elevator button. She glanced back at Annie who was staring at her, her smile gone. The woman turned and started tapping on the keyboard. Toni stepped onto the elevator.

Annie seemed almost hostile about Jade as if she blamed her for the entire incident as Olivia called it.

Toni wondered what really happened to Jade on Tuesday. Were Olivia and Annie trying to protect someone else by downplaying Jade's assault?

Chapter 8

Saturday, June 10 at 1:10 pm

She had only been to Cam's house once when he moved in about a year ago. Cori managed to recruit her to help with the move. It turned out to be a lot of fun that day. Today's visit wasn't going to be quite as memorable. She hated to bother him on a Saturday, but there was no way she could keep what she learned to herself all weekend.

Cam lived in a quiet neighborhood that was fifteen minutes from downtown Charlotte. She wasn't too surprised that Cam became a cop. He'd hung over at their house on many occasions with Cori. Growing up without his dad around, Justice Reed became Cam's surrogate father. Cam really was like another brother. He teased her just as much as her own brother, which she didn't mind.

She'd enjoyed his attention, but she never wanted Cam to know how much she really liked him.

When Cam went off to play football at Florida State, they all grew apart. Later when he returned to Charlotte after a short stint in the NFL, he and Cori picked up their friendship. She kept her distance mainly because Cam always seemed to have a girlfriend. Plus, Cam was just her brother's best friend. Nothing more.

Right now as she rang Cam's doorbell, Toni hoped she was not jeopardizing her own friendship.

Cam opened the door dressed in a Carolina Panthers t-shirt and jeans. "Hey, what a surprise."

Toni smiled trying to keep from staring at Cam's muscular arms. "I hope I'm not disturbing you."

He frowned. "Not at all. I'm always happy to see you. Come on back. I'm working in my shop, if that's okay."

"I forgot you had plans to setup a woodworking shop in the garage. So, you did it?" Toni stepped inside. Cam's style was contemporary. His dark wood floors stretched from his sleek living room back to his state-of-the art kitchen. She followed him through the kitchen out to his two-car garage.

On one side of the garage, his old Camaro sat

covered. On the other side, Cam had built in shelves to hold his woodworking tools. Lined up on other shelves were various creations.

She nodded. "I'm impressed."

He grinned. "I finished the setup about three months ago. Turned out to be a great winter project. Me and you really need to hang out more."

Now, why would he say that?

Toni's face grew warm. She walked away from him to examine the items on the counter. Her embarrassment forgotten, she picked up a wooden train and turned around to face him. "This is gorgeous. Are you selling any of these?"

Cam shrugged. "Not really. I've been giving some of them away at Christmas and other times of the year to a few children's charities."

"These would sell well on Etsy."

"Etsy?"

"It's an e-commerce platform for people who like to create and sell handmade items. Really, you can sell a variety of things. My store is how I get a lot of customers."

"Well, maybe you can help me get setup. It would be a good excuse to hang out."

Toni's face burned. *Is Cam seriously flirting with me?*

She placed the train back on the counter. He would change his tune soon. Toni crossed her arms and sighed.

Cam looked at her. "You didn't come by today to talk about my side projects. What's on your mind, Toni? You look like something is troubling you."

"Yea. Remember the other day you mentioned Paul had a fiancée?"

Cam nodded slowly. "Yes."

"I met her. Olivia Niles."

He blew out a breath as though he needed to prepare himself. "Why did you go see Ms. Niles? Do you really think that was a good idea?"

Toni said, "I told her my name. She didn't seem to make any connection, not unless she just didn't know that I knew Paul."

Cam's eyes opened wide. "What if she shares your name with Paul?"

"It wasn't my plan to see her. I went there to reach out to Jade."

Cam rubbed his temple. "This is not sounding any better. Why would you want to see Jade? Wait, why am I asking? This kind of thing runs in your family."

She ignored Cam's sarcasm. "If you're saying I'm having trouble letting go of what's bothering me...

Guilty. I don't see how Jade couldn't have known Paul due to the fact that she works for his fiancée."

Cam frowned, "I don't think Jade is on the payroll. She's a volunteer. I've seen the volunteer list. It's not a small listing."

"Still, she should know something about Olivia. If Jade manages the social media, you can't miss them as a couple." Toni paced the garage floor with her arms crossed. "I also saw the area where Jade was attacked. Olivia kind of swept it under the rug."

Cam grimaced. "I'm sure Ms. Niles didn't want to draw attention to a *stranger* that a woman was attacked on the premises. Her foundation is about helping women. At this point, she's protecting the foundation's reputation. When we released the composite to the media, she requested discretion."

Toni asked, "I understand all that. I just thought she still should've been more empathetic. Jade was volunteering at her fundraiser event. Speaking of the crime scene area, I assume there are DNA samples."

Cam let out a deep sigh. "What is with the third degree here? Yes, we took Jade's clothes. Unfortunately, the office was used by quite a few people so investigators had a hard time finding any distinguishing fingerprints that didn't belong."

"What about the cameras?"

Cam stared at her. "You really went to the Niles Foundation on a quest."

"It wasn't my plan. Remember, I'm used to listening to my siblings talk. It was natural to look for cameras. If the gallery had valuables, surely there would be security."

Cam shifted on his feet like he didn't really feel like talking anymore.

Toni knew she should probably stop with her questions, but she couldn't resist asking. "What else do you know about Jade?"

Cam rubbed his hands across his head. "Did you seriously come here to ask me to look into the victim? You of all people should be on the *victim's* side. The woman *was* assaulted. And a valuable painting was stolen."

Toni paused. "I wonder how someone pulled that off." She quickly added, "I'm not saying that something didn't happen to Jade."

"Then what are you trying to accomplish with your little investigation?"

She'd never heard that tone of voice from Cam before. Toni observed Cam before responding.

"I see I've stepped over the line here. I'm sorry. This was obviously as you said a robbery. I was just confused. Jade flat out told me she was the social media manager. The receptionist, Annie, said she was just a volunteer. She embellished her role at the Niles Foundation. Why?"

"Toni, that's not a reason to be questioning the victim. It wasn't her fault she left her phone and someone happened to be in the building up to no good."

"Something just doesn't feel right. Jade doesn't seem to be telling the whole truth. Doesn't that strike you as strange? Am I being silly here thinking there's more to this whole thing?"

Cam threw up his hands, "Sorry, I thought I was the detective on this case. I'm baffled why you have such an interest. I told you Paul had an alibi. Unfortunately, no one has come forward about the composite yet. But this... Toni, it's like you're on a mission to find a way to pin this on Paul Lambert."

"No, I'm not. I know you said he wasn't there, but then I find out the woman who planned the whole event is his fiancée. She has control of the guest list."

"So now you're accusing Olivia Niles of hiding the fact that her fiancé was in the building?"

"Well, it's possible." She responded under her breath.

"Toni, in order for someone's alibi to check out, they have to prove their whereabouts. Paul was with Olivia around the same time Jade was assaulted. He picked up Olivia after the fundraiser about thirty minutes before the crime took place. They have witnesses to verify they both left together in his car. The others stayed around to clean up before heading home."

Toni's mind raced. *Did Paul come back?*

Cam walked closer to her. "Lets talk this through, okay? Because I can tell you're not convinced."

She looked at Cam thinking he knew her too well. That kind of surprised her.

Cam held up two fingers. "The facts. Number one, the person who was in the building had no intentions of committing an assault that night. He waited until everyone left the building for a reason. He wanted to get into that gallery. He was successful. Two, I believe Jade surprised him. Maybe he thought she saw him in the act. I don't know. He tried to strangle her, which makes this more than an assault. Closer to attempted murder. Pretty serious, you agree?"

Toni nodded for Cam to continue.

"We both know Paul is a wealthy man. The Lambert family is well known. Even if Paul didn't have an alibi, what's his motive for ripping off his fiancée?"

Cam crossed his arms and stared at her.

Toni looked away. She felt really stupid now and stared at the floor. "I guess I needed you to lay it out for me. What do I know? I just sketch faces."

Still a question lingered. "Don't throw anything at me, but what about all those cameras? You're saying someone stole a painting and a woman was assaulted. Sounds like the security company needs to be fired."

That made Cam crack a smile. "I have to agree with you. Someone either hacked into the security system or this was an inside job. Right now, I'm hoping there are some electronic footprints."

"On the footage we have, most of the guests left by ten o'clock. Olivia and her staff closed up the gallery around eleven. Maybe ten minutes after eleven, Mr. Lambert picked up Ms. Niles. The only person we saw re-entering the building was Jade, who as you know forgot her phone. The one area where cameras are not located is around the office where Jade was attacked. But the strange thing is the cameras seemed to show some type of loop."

"They setup a way for this person to get what they wanted from the gallery. I was thinking they entered and left by going down the stairwell."

Cam arched his eyebrow. "Good catch, detective-in-training. Could be true. None of the cameras on the other floors were tampered with that we could tell. We talked to the guard downstairs. He saw nothing on his round. He or she knew how to work their way around the building undetected."

Toni frowned, "He or she?"

Cam nodded. "I know Jade worked with you on the sketch, but I've been doing this long enough to not pay attention to all details. Only women who worked in that office had the ability to move in and out of the gallery. Plus, this robbery had to be at least a two-person job."

More than one person.

Toni asked, "I'm assuming you're looking at all foundation employees and that long volunteer list."

"You betcha. Detective work is not easy."

Toni knew she had more questions than answers, but she felt like she had only succeeded in offending Cam. "I'm sorry for bringing this to you on a Saturday when you're trying to relax. You shared way more than you should have."

He shrugged. "My cases never quite leave me alone. I was here in the shop late last night thinking about the case, especially since I don't have leads. Whoever was there, they got what they wanted which is causing a whole lot of other issues. It would be nice if that painting showed up somewhere or if we could figure out who tampered with the security system."

They stood in silence for a few minutes.

Cam interrupted the silence. "Toni, I could be out of line here, but have you really dealt with what Paul did to you? Did you ever go for counseling?"

Toni caught her breath not expecting the rush of tears that came to her eyes. Now Cam was questioning her. "My issues have nothing to do with the fact that there are some sketchy details on this case."

"That's not what I'm saying. I'm just concerned that you may be projecting some unreleased emotions in the wrong direction."

"That's not true. I helped a victim place a face for her attacker. I want the right person arrested and convicted. I've been living my life just fine."

That wasn't really true.

It was time for her to go. "I'm sorry for bothering you. I promise to stay out of your investigation." She moved towards the kitchen door.

"Toni, stop." Cam leapt in front of her. "Don't leave like this. I don't want this to keep bothering you. A man is supposed to protect the woman he claims to love, not hurt her. Paul hurt you."

"Yes, he did. I don't want him to ever hurt anyone else."

He reached out and touched her arm. "Paul Lambert has moved on and you can do the same. I'm going to pray that you can truly move forward."

"Thank you." Toni was touched by Cam's offer to pray for her and without thinking she reached her arms around him, feeling the firmness of his back muscles as she hugged him. She laid her head against his chest.

He held her. For a brief moment her mind focused on how good it felt to be in Cam's arms.

She stepped back reluctantly and mumbled, "Sorry."

Cam observed her, "I'm not sorry."

His eyes held hers. Toni looked away. "I really do need to go."

"You can head out this way to your car."

She watched as Cam pressed the garage door opener. When the door lifted, she stepped out into the heat towards her car. After climbing inside, she waved at Cam, who stood watching her from inside the garage.

As she drove away, her mind focused on the embrace with Cam.

Hmm...that felt so right. I needed that.

Another thought broke her euphoria.

I wonder what Olivia's reaction was when Cam showed her the composite? Surely she would've noticed some resemblance to Paul.

Toni blew out a breath. It didn't matter. She hadn't told Cam about her meeting with Olivia next week, one she had no intentions of canceling.

She didn't understand if it was her curiosity or something else, but Toni still wanted to know more about the woman Paul was marrying.

Chapter 9

Sunday, June 11 at 3:14 pm

Sundays were pretty important to Toni. After the week she'd had, spending worship time with her family was exactly what she needed. Toni attended service at Victory Gospel Church and sat with Jo's family. She glanced over to see Jo's husband, Bryan, with his arms around her sister and smiled. It looked like her sister's marriage wasn't going to fall apart despite Bryan's affair last fall. Now with the new baby girl coming, her sister and brother-in-law seemed to be back on track. Her nephew, B.J., squirmed beside her before eventually laying his head on her shoulder.

Since their parents were out of town, Sunday dinner was at Jo's house. Bryan had baked his famous lasagna while Jo pulled together a salad. It wasn't the Southern cooking they were all used to from their mom, but both Cori and Toni, the non-cooks of the family were happy for a home-cooked meal. Toni still had hopes of being a wife and mom one day soon. Some day it would be her turn to host Sunday dinner for her family.

As Bryan and Jo cleared the table, Toni grabbed her phone and walked outside to the patio. Her sister's backyard was an oasis with flowers bordering the yard. Bryan kept the grass immaculate with a weekly cut. Toni settled into one of the cushioned chairs and stared at the trees that separated the yard from the neighboring yard. Her mind still whirled with questions, no matter how much she tried to switch gears.

In the distance, she heard Cori chasing B.J. Her thoughts slipped to Cam and their embrace yesterday.

I'm not ready.

Cam was right. She had a lot more emotional baggage to unpack.

She turned to see her sister Jo squeeze her growing stomach through the door opening.

"Hey, you enjoy dinner?" Jo eased into the other patio chair.

Toni smiled. "Of course, I always appreciate

Bryan's lasagna." She patted her stomach. "My tummy is happy."

Jo grinned. "I appreciate not having to cook. Didn't you say you had something to show me?"

After the assault, Toni had started painting images that flooded her mind during her recovery. In a matter of four weeks, she had painted seven different pieces all showing a woman in various stages of pain. The watercolor collection was very different for her. She ended up storing the paintings in the back of her closet and moving on to other projects.

She'd never showed the paintings to her family. At least until now. Toni had taken photos of the paintings last night with her phone. She passed her phone to Jo and twisted her fingers as she waited for her sister's response.

After a few minutes, Jo looked up with tears in her eyes. "These are beautiful. You had these hidden all this time?"

Toni nodded. "I guess I wasn't ready to show them yet."

Her brother stepped out on the patio. "B.J. must of have had a busy weekend. He went down for a nap in no time." He looked back and forth between

Jo and Cori. "Uh oh. Girl talk, maybe I need to head back inside."

"You should see Toni's paintings." Jo passed the phone to him.

Toni rubbed her hands together as her twin quietly flipped through the photos. Cori handed the phone to Toni. "Sis, these paintings are stunning. So what are you planning to do with these?"

Even after her conversation with Cam yesterday, Toni still felt led to share the collection with Olivia. "I met up with a foundation that supports causes for women. I'm meeting with them on Tuesday to see if they're interested. If so, I'm willing to donate the pieces for a good cause."

Jo clasped her hands over her belly. "I'm so proud of you. It's like a step towards your healing. That's what I see in those pieces. The first three have a lot of pain, but there is a transition to peace by the time you view the last one."

Toni swallowed. "Maybe this is my way of getting to that last transition."

Jo stood and hugged her. "Good for you, sis. It's time for you to be happy. You deserve it."

As Jo headed back towards the kitchen, Cori plopped on the chair next to her. "Cam called last night. Said I should make sure you stay out of trouble. Any particular reason why?"

Toni arched her eye. "What else did he say?"

"Nothing. Just that I should probably keep an eye on you."

Her warm feelings towards Cam changed. *Did he really think he was being helpful by talking to her brother?*

"I'm okay, Cori. Cam and I had a heart to heart talk yesterday and I'm moving forward, staying out of his way."

Cori narrowed his eyes. "This still has to do with that composite that resembled Paul?"

She shook her head. "It's apparently not Paul. He has an alibi. So, no worries."

"Really? Because you've been awfully quiet today. Not just today, all week."

"Cam is a good detective. I know he's covering all the bases. There's just some details that are bugging me."

"Like what? I don't need you and Cam having a falling out."

"It's not like that. We're cool."

"Good because you know he really likes you." Cori widened his eyes. "A lot."

Toni whipped her head and looked at her brother. "What?"

"Oh, come on. Don't tell me you haven't noticed? When we were kids, he wasn't coming around all the time just to hang out with me. I always caught him looking at you. His eyes going all soft."

"Stop playing." She didn't believe what she was hearing, but she couldn't wipe the smile off her face. "He never asked me out."

"Probably because he was afraid too. I mean I wasn't the one getting in the way, but Dad is kind of intimidating you know."

"Still, we're older now. Dad isn't an issue."

"You're right about that. I don't know. I guess he's still working his nerve up. Or either he thinks you're not interested. Are you?"

"I..." She thought of the hug again. She was definitely interested, but she wasn't sure if this was the right time.

Cori interrupted her thoughts. "You're still shackled down by what Paul did to you. When are you going to get past that, Toni?"

"I'm doing it now."

"Well, I hope you are because I need you and

Cam to stop walking around each other like you're on eggshells."

Toni thought back to her conversation with Cam on Saturday. He was comforting to her despite the fact she practically accused him of not doing his job. He didn't have to share the details of the case with her like he did. He was truly looking out for her.

She looked at Cori. "I do have a question for you."

"Uh oh. Is this a work-related question?"

"Yeah. Which you know you like to answer because you're such a nerd?"

Cori rolled his eyes. "Whatever. Ask away."

"If you were planning to rob a place and you knew it had really good security, is there a way to hack the cameras?"

Cori arched his eyebrows at her. "Uhmm, where are we going with this conversation?"

"It's about this case. Just tell me."

"Of course it's possible. I guess if I wanted to get into a place, I would definitely look at the timing. You can probably hack into the system and take into account what's going on during that time of day. Based on a certain time period, you could replace the actual cameras with a recording. So anyone who's looking at the screen would see what you wanted them to see."

"So, a thief could get inside a place and get what they wanted undetected by the cameras?"

"Yeah. In most of those really cool heist movies, that's what always happens. The key is you have to do it in a certain amount of time without raising suspicion."

A theory started whirling in Toni's mind, but she still couldn't quite place her finger on why.

It all came back to Jade Lewis. There wasn't anything wrong with forgetting one's phone. It happens. Still, Toni became increasingly curious about Jade and knew at some point she wanted to talk to her again.

She would have to do it without Cam's knowledge.

Chapter 10

Tuesday, June 13 at 9:51 am

Toni took a deep breath as she watched the elevator rise to number three. She held tight to her portfolio case. Even after her siblings encouraged her to move forward with sharing her collection, she still questioned if this was the right thing to do. This woman was Paul's fiancée. She'd really expected the appointment to be cancelled, but no such call or email came.

She stepped off the elevator into the familiar lobby. Annie looked up and her smiled faltered. "Ms. Reed. You're early."

Toni hesitated as she walked up to the desk. "I hope that's okay."

Annie grimaced. "It may be awhile. Liv has a disgruntled person in her office at the moment.

Have a seat over in our waiting area. I'll let you know when Olivia can see you."

"I'm sorry to hear that. I can't imagine you would ever have anyone like that with the foundation's worthy causes."

Annie rolled her eyes. "Believe me, when people donate," she made curly quotes with her fingers as she said the word donate, "they are very particular about how you spend their money. Not that Liv would do anything wrong."

Toni nodded. She sat in a comfortable high-back chair in the waiting room and pulled out her phone to scan her emails, her mind full of questions. At least twenty minutes passed. A man marched out into the hallway.

Toni turned to see a short balding man with a red face. "I really hope you can find that painting. My late wife loved that artist and that particular painting."

"Mr. Stewart, I'm so sorry. The police are doing everything they can to locate it."

The man stabbed the elevator button. "Well, you should know if they don't find it, I cannot follow suit with the donation."

Olivia looked like she was going to burst into tears as she watched Mr. Stewart enter the elevator.

She walked over to Annie and wailed, "This is horrible. We can't afford to lose $10,000. Call that detective. See if he's found out anything yet."

Wow, Toni thought. *That's a lot of money for a painting.*

Toni stood to catch Liv's attention, "This seems like a bad time. Maybe we should reschedule?"

Olivia twirled around. "Toni. I'm sorry to keep you waiting. It's been a busy morning. A really terrible morning."

"Not a problem," Toni held up her phone. "Always something to do on the phone. Look, I appreciate your interest, but maybe…"

Olivia grinned, "No, I want to see your paintings. I need something good to happen today."

Annie appeared concern. "Are you sure you should take on another appointment today?"

Olivia waved at her secretary. "I'm fine." Looking back at Toni, she said, "Follow me back to my office."

Toni trailed Olivia down the hallway in the opposite direction of the gallery. When she walked into Olivia's office, she was impressed with the size. There was a mini conference area on one side and on the other side there was a couch and chairs. Behind Olivia's expansive desk was a view of Charlotte's downtown. "What a great view. I love your workspace."

"Thank you. The owner of this building and the interior designer were both friends of my mother. My mom hasn't been with us for about five years now, but so many people who knew her have helped us build this foundation in her name."

"I'm sure she'd be proud of all the work you've done with the foundation."

"I hope so. It certainly has been rewarding...until now. I don't know what happened last week."

Toni hedged, "The robbery and assault?"

Olivia looked at her. "Yes. I feel bad for the volunteer. I don't know who would have targeted my gallery. I mean we have the best security system."

"If you don't mind me saying, you've been really nice and forthcoming with me and we don't even know each other. Are you always so nice?"

Olivia blushed. "It's the way I am. My mom used to tell me I'm too trusting. Too nice." She shook her body like she was trying to shake away something hanging on her. "Enough of me and my issues. I knew there was something about you when we met last week. It felt like we've known

each other forever. Let's see your collection. You can lay it on this table."

Like she's known me forever.

Toni stalled for a minute, took a deep breath and walked over to the table. She opened the case and stepped back, standing with her arms crossed as Olivia flipped through the portfolio observing each painting.

"My, my. Toni, these are breathtaking. I can really feel the pain in these first few pieces. I love the use of the various tones of blue. They feel so personal."

Toni looked at Olivia. It was time to come clean. At least a little. "They're very personal. I was assaulted by a man I thought I loved. He hurt me pretty bad. I spent a few days in the hospital and months afterward recovering from my injuries. As soon as I could handle a paintbrush, that's how I tried to get through my healing process. I don't think I was ready at the time to show anyone so I stored them away."

Olivia stared at Toni. She spoke quietly. "I'm so sorry to hear about your ordeal. Men can be really cruel. Are you sure you're ready to share these with the world?"

Toni wasn't sure about the *world* part. Her

assault and trial were in the news. She was happy when it was over despite the outcome. "I'm ready. Maybe they will speak to someone else's pain."

"You know it would be so wonderful for you to share your story. I can see us doing an event, but I would want you to be a part of it. Hearing your story like you just told me with the paintings hanging in the gallery would be perfect.

Toni wasn't expecting all of that. "I'm not much of a public speaker."

"Oh, we can coach you. Most of the women we work with are not public speakers and they have a lot of hesitation too. Just think about it. I usually like to start planning six to nine months in advance. We start planning our breast cancer awareness fundraiser in January, even though the event is in October. I could do something on a smaller scale as a start probably towards the end of October for domestic violence. What do you think?"

"Can I think about it?"

"Sure, but don't take too long. Once we get the ball rolling, I want to do some photo shoots probably in late July so we can pull the promotional pieces together and have them out in September."

Toni's face warmed. This was not going to go well and she knew it. She'd come to meet Olivia under dual purposes.

Would Olivia be this enthusiastic if she knew her fiancé was responsible for the creation of these paintings?

Toni remarked, "I can learn a lot of business marketing from you."

"That's right. You're self-employed. Do you make all your business from your paintings?"

"Oh no. I've adapted some of my paintings to prints and those have merchandise behind them. Last week, I launched a jewelry line." Toni held out her arm. "This is one of my bracelets."

Olivia leaned over. "Oh my! You are quite the artist. That's beautiful."

"You can look me up on Instagram. I have plenty of samples. Speaking of Instagram, Jade does a great job with the foundation's account."

Olivia frowned. "Jade? You mean Carol. I hate to say this but Carol, our social media manager, is so good I pay her to manage my personal social media accounts too."

"That's interesting. I talked to a woman named Jade. I believe she volunteers here."

Olivia's smile disappeared. "Um, I should know

her, but I get super-focused with our donors. Annie has more of a relationship with our volunteers."

"I see. Does Carol work with other people? Maybe she outsources?"

Olivia frowned. "I don't know. Carol is such a powerhouse. It's possible she could have a small team that she delegates to. I wouldn't know. I'm just grateful for her keeping me relevant online."

"Does she take other clients?"

"I'm sure she does. I'm not sure how she keeps up with all the accounts, but she's really good. Here, let me give you her information. Most of the time she works remote from her home. She has three year old and a one year old so how she keeps it all together is her secret."

Toni folded her portfolio as Olivia jotted Carol's information on a yellow legal pad. She was puzzled that Olivia didn't seem to connect Jade to being the volunteer who was assaulted last week inside her offices.

Or was this another effort to keep the incident low key?

Olivia ripped the paper off the pad and handed it to Toni. "I hope Carol can help you. I do keep her pretty busy."

Toni reached for the paper. She folded the paper and placed it in the side pocket of her bag. "Thank you. I appreciate your time."

"My pleasure. I'm so excited for the opportunity to introduce you and your work to others. I appreciate your willingness to share your healing process after what happened to you. Did the man who hurt you ever get charged?"

Toni grimaced. "He got a light sentence. Rehabilitation. Restraining order. Hopefully, he learned from his ways and won't hurt anyone else."

Something flickered in Olivia's eyes. Toni couldn't tell if it was fear or empathy for her story.

Whatever it was, it passed as Olivia extended her hand. "I'll be in touch in a few weeks to see if you want to pursue the event."

Toni shook Olivia's hand. "Thank you for your time. I'll give the idea some thought." She grabbed her portfolio and turned to leave the office.

She nodded at Annie as she walked over to the elevator and punched the button. Toni wasn't sure if her visit was worthwhile.

When the elevator door opened, her hands turned icy cold as she gripped her portfolio case.

Oh no, I knew I shouldn't have done this.

Toni exchanged stares with Paul Lambert before he stepped out of the elevator.

"Toni?" His voice sounded surprised. "It's been a long time."

"Yes. It has. Excuse me." She moved past him into the elevator and stabbed the button for the lobby floor. She prayed the elevator doors would close quickly. Toni wouldn't look in his direction, but she felt the intensity of Paul's stare. Before the doors closed, she caught a fleeting glimpse of Olivia walking up behind Paul.

When the elevator doors shut, her body began to shake.

Stirring up trouble was precisely what Cam had warned her not to do.

Chapter 11

Tuesday, June 13 at 12:06 pm

Toni drove back to her apartment in a panic. She was still in shock at seeing Paul in person. There was no reason for him to think that it was anything other than a coincidence about her being there. Still, she wondered if he would say something to Olivia.

Would that be so bad? Maybe Olivia needed to know who she was engaged to marry.

Toni pulled up to her apartment and sat in the car with the air condition running for a while so she wouldn't suffocate in the summer heat. She didn't like deceit. The whole point of showing her collection to Olivia was so she could share her healing process with others. She really didn't want to lose that opportunity now. She slapped the steering wheel and turned the car off.

Once inside her apartment, she leaned her portfolio against the coffee table, dropped her bag on the floor and plopped on the couch. She sat in silence with her arms folded for several moments before glancing at her bag.

Toni reached into the side pocket and pulled out the paper Olivia had scribbled Carol Landers's contact information on. She may need to drop the foundation opportunity for now to avoid Paul, but she still had lingering questions. Her whole intention for going to the Niles Foundation last week was to talk to Jade again. Here Toni was running into people she didn't need to be seeing and she still hadn't made contact with Jade.

So what was her story?

It appeared Carol Landers was the connection to Jade.

She reached back in her bag and pulled out her phone. After staring at the paper for a minute, she tapped the numbers. Toni waited as the phone rang on the other end.

"Hello."

Toni sat up. "Hello, is this Carol Landers?"

"Yes, this is she. Can I help you?"

"I'm in need of a social media manager. Olivia Niles referred me to you."

"Oh wow. Well certainly, if Olivia referred you, you're good people. Olivia rarely sends me clients."

"She said you're really good."

"I do what I can. What type of social media platforms are you on?"

"Facebook and Twitter, but I really need help with my Instagram. I have tons of photos that a friend helped me take and it's just hard to remember to post them. I have a Pinterest account I started, but I never remember to update it."

"Well, I can certainly help you with that. I manage a few Instagram and Pinterest accounts. Are you a photographer?"

"An artist. I have photos of my artwork and jewelry designs. So, how do we get started? Do we need to meet in person?"

"It's not necessary. I do everything remotely, but I don't have anything against meeting in person as long as you're local. "

"I'm in Charlotte and I'm free anytime this week."

"Awesome. How about we meet on Friday at Park Place Mall. Let's say 11:00 am?"

"Perfect."

"What's your usernames for your accounts so I can take a look?"

"All my accounts are under my name Toni with an 'i.' My last name is Reed. Toni Reed."

"Okay, great. I will take a look tonight and I look forward to talking to you on Friday."

"Sounds good. Goodbye."

Toni hung up the phone and laid it on the table. She wasn't sure where anything was going lately. What she did know was she had her own business to run. Even more importantly, she needed to feed her stomach. She got up, went into the kitchen and opened the fridge. Empty. She should have taken time to go to the grocery store. There was only so much eating out she could do.

After scrounging through her cabinets, she settled on peanut butter and crackers. No wonder her mom and sisters complained about her weight. She didn't eat worth two cents.

She grabbed a water bottle. As she chomped on her crackers, she noticed her phone screen had lit up.

Who is calling me?

With a mouthful of crackers, Toni went over to the phone and picked it up. Whoever had called left a message. She didn't recognize the phone number though.

Maybe it was Carol calling back on another number.

Toni placed another cracker in her mouth and pressed the voicemail.

She froze as she listened to the familiar voice.

"What do you think you're doing? Haven't you done enough to me already? Now you're going to show up in my life again. Stay away from 'Liv. Leave me alone!"

Paul!

His voice was tight with anger. Just like *that* day.

Her mouth felt like it was stuck. She forgot she'd been chewing and found herself trying to swallow. She wrenched the cap off the water bottle and guzzled the water. With shaking hands, she held onto the kitchen chair until she caught her breath. Her heart was beating so fast.

Did Paul forget? He wasn't supposed to contact her. Just because they ran into each other today, didn't give him the right to violate his order.

As she calmed her frazzled nerves, it occurred to her that Paul seemed awfully focused on her not having contact with his fiancée.

Did that mean Olivia was really clueless about Paul's past?

Toni always prayed that no one else would feel Paul's wrath. Now she wondered if there were other reasons why she had crossed paths with Olivia.

Chapter 12

Thursday, June 15 at 12:06 pm

Toni stayed to herself after getting the voicemail from Paul. If anything came of her meeting with Olivia and her foundation, maybe she would at least get a social media manager. Toni gathered her accounts and emailed them to Carol. She left the paintings sitting in the corner of the living room, although she was tempted to stick them back inside the closet again.

Her parents had returned to town late Wednesday afternoon. Determined to get out of the house on Thursday, she headed to her childhood home. There was nothing quite like sitting in her parent's kitchen. As she watched her mom and dad banter back and forth, Toni felt the most normal she'd felt in a few days. It was good to have them back home.

"That's the last time I'll be getting out on the water again. My legs still feel funny."

Toni smiled. "Dad, you'll be fine. Your legs are adjusting to being back on land. You both looked so tanned and rested."

Vanessa Reed smiled. "Don't listen to him. We had a great time. I must admit I had reservations about being on a big boat and we did have a rocky ride one night, but I enjoyed myself." She winked. "We will be doing another cruise."

Justice Reed grinned. "She was like a wild woman. We were on the go all day and all night. I'm glad to be home and now I'm going to rest these old sea legs."

Vanessa turned to Toni. "So, how have you been? I'm surprised I didn't hear a peep from my baby girl while we were gone."

Toni frowned. "Mama, I wasn't going to bother you on your vacation."

Her mother peered at her. "But something is bothering you. You have that look you had when you were a little girl and you were worried about something."

Toni shook her head. It was impossible to keep

anything from her mama. Still, she didn't know if she wanted to reveal anything about last week. If anything, she wished she could just move on. "I don't know where to start, Mama."

"Just start with what's on your mind or better yet what I hear about these secret paintings."

"I guess they're not a secret anymore. I just didn't want to reveal them for awhile." Toni pulled up the photos of her collection on her phone and showed them to her mom. She sat, anxiously awaiting feedback.

Her mom looked at her. Her eyes glistened. "These are beautiful. Just to think so much beauty from so much pain. It's like that verse, "Beauty for ashes.""

"Thanks, Mama. I don't know why I put those in the back of the closet all this time."

"Because maybe you needed time to forgive yourself. It's like you've been beating yourself up over being with that man. None of us know what we're walking into when we start a new relationship."

"Yeah, but you and everyone else tried to warn me. I knew there were times God gave me warning signs and I ignored them."

"We're all guilty of not wanting to see what's

in front of us. The point is, I think now you're listening, really listening to God. He's trying to draw you out so you won't miss what He has for you. What seemed like a really bad thing is going to be for some good now."

"I hope so. This past week has been a bit confusing."

"You were on my mind while we were away. Not that I wasn't thinking about my other children too, but I sensed something was going on. You ready to talk about it?"

Her mother may have been thousands of miles away, but the radar was clearly working.

Toni leaned back in the chair and crossed her arms. She'd only really shared details of her reaction to the composite with Cori. She wasn't sure if she wanted to share everything else that had happened, but if there was anyone she usually spilled her thoughts too, it was Mama.

There weren't too many secrets in the Reed family either.

She sighed deeply. "Okay. It all started last week when Cam asked me to draw a composite for an assault case. I'm sure he regrets asking me now."

Her mom smiled, "I doubt Cam regrets anything that concerns you, Toni. He's pretty protective."

Toni rolled her eyes. "Mama, no matchmaking."

"I'm just saying."

"Anyway, I have probably been sticking my nose where it doesn't belong, but I know something's not right with this case."

"That just means you're a Reed. All of you have those inquisitive minds. When something is bothering any of you, you become a bit obsessed with figuring out the pieces of the puzzle."

"Well certain pieces aren't fitting together." Toni paused. "You should know my first reaction to the composite after it was completed was that the face reminded me of Paul."

Vanessa's eyes shot up. "Paul Lambert? You're saying he assaulted this woman. He didn't learn?"

"Wait, hold up. Paul supposedly has an alibi, but that's not all."

"Oh?"

"His alibi is from his fiancée, Olivia Niles. She created the Niles Foundation."

Her mother frowned. "This is the place you're thinking of donating your paintings?"

"Yes. Also the place where the assault took place last week."

"What?"

"Yes. You haven't heard all of it either. I ran into

Paul while he was coming to visit Olivia on Tuesday. It was a surprise seeing him after almost two years. He wasn't pleased to see me and he let me know that later."

"He contacted you. He's not supposed to do that."

"You're right. He's not. But, I unintentionally set myself up to be in a place where he could show up too."

"My, my, young lady, what have you gotten yourself into? Now I'm not so sure about you being involved with this foundation. Does anyone else know what you've been up to?"

"Just Cam and believe me he's given me plenty of warnings. Alibi or no alibi, I'm not convinced that Olivia isn't protecting Paul somehow. On the other hand, the victim is a strange woman."

Her mama frowned. "You sound like you don't believe her. Wasn't she assaulted?"

"Yes, there's no doubt she was assaulted because she had injuries. It's just something about her." Toni stood up. "I feel bad about that because I've been in her place. I've been a victim."

Vanessa shook her head. "Well, no matter what her story is she still needs the person found who assaulted her. Whether it turns out to be Paul or not, that's Cam's job. You don't need anymore run-ins with Paul Lambert. By the way, did you renew the protective order yet?"

"You know about that?"

"You know you didn't call while we were on the cruise, but your sisters did keep in touch. That's one of the reasons why you were on my mind. I expected you to call. I know when I don't hear from you that you have a tendency to lean towards...well, trouble."

Toni frowned. "Really?"

Vanessa crossed her arms. "You know what alarmed everyone the most when you were with Paul?"

Toni shook her head.

"You shut us out. You went from being the one who was always concerned about everyone to being very withdrawn."

"I didn't think I was doing that. I could tell y'all didn't approve of him."

Vanessa sucked in a sharp breath. "I'm glad God brought you out of that relationship safely. It could have been a lot worse." Her mama pointed her finger. "You need to keep your distance from Paul. I know you have good intentions, but I think you need to pray more on whether or not you should even be involved with that woman and her foundation. She's way too close to Paul."

Toni closed her eyes. "I will."

Vanessa walked over and hugged her. She stood back. "I mean it when I say pray. It's obvious you've reached a point of healing. This is a crucial time because the adversary will steal your progress and tempt you to fall backwards. God will send other opportunities to you."

Toni knew her mother was right. She still was puzzled by Paul's comment.

Stay away from 'Liv. Leave me alone!

It was more than just his comment. It was the desperate tone of frustration in his voice. She hadn't seen him in two years. The man barely received any punishment for assaulting her, his business was still going strong and he was engaged to a beautiful woman.

Why did Paul react so intensely towards seeing me in person?

Chapter 13

Friday, June 16 at 11:36 am

How Carol Landers kept up with anything with her two young children boggled Toni's mind. She watched the frazzled woman try to quiet her squirming one-year-old daughter who was anything but happy to be sitting on her mother's lap. The toddler had tried to take off running several times. After the toddler was consoled with a juice bottle, Toni watched in amazement as the woman used her other free hand to stop her three-year-old son from pulling napkins from the dispenser.

Carol appeared embarrassed. "I'm so sorry. My cousin usually helps me with the kids, but she went missing-in-action this morning. To be honest, I don't think she made it home last night so I'm extra worried. I promise you my life does not look like this and I can *manage* your social media."

Toni shook her head. "Not a problem. Good help can be hard to find. I babysat for my sister so I know this age can be a handful."

Carol wiped her son's hands now covered in ketchup. "I really don't want you to think I'm not competent. I am. Once we work out a plan on the types of posts, I can get a system in place and it will run like a well-oiled machine."

"Olivia gave you a really high recommendation. I imagine working from home helps with caring for the little ones."

"Oh it's been a blessing to be able to stay at home with the kids and have this to do on the side. The work keeps me sane." Carol laughed from her belly.

Toni smiled. She liked Carol. But from what she saw, Toni couldn't help but wonder. "Do you keep up with all of your clients' accounts by yourself or do you get help sometimes?"

Carol blew her bangs off her face as she moved the younger child to her other arm. "I do have help sometimes, especially this last year with giving birth to Jenny here. I didn't want to lose my clients so I got some help. I can assure you Landers

Publicity never misses a beat with keeping your social media active."

"That sounds great. So, I understand you manage the Instagram account for Olivia. I like what you do with the quotes over the photos. Is that something you can do for me?"

"Sure, that's not a problem at all." Carol suddenly looked like a deer with headlights in her eyes as loud ringing exploded from the phone on the table. She looked at the phone. "I'm sorry. I need to get this. This may be my rescue."

Toni nodded and drank her coffee as Carol took the call. From Carol's desperate pleas, Toni gathered she had touched base with her cousin.

A few moments later, Carol took a deep breath, "Help is on the way. My cousin finally showed up. She should be here in a few minutes. She said she wasn't that far away."

Toni offered, "Why don't we go walking? I remember my sister used to try that to taper her son's energy a notch."

"Good idea."

Toni helped Carol get both toddlers settled into the double stroller.

As they walked, Toni asked, "Tell me how you got started at the Niles Foundation."

"Well, Olivia and I have been friends since college. When her mother passed away from breast cancer, she was really depressed. She and her mother were more like sisters. It was just the two of them for so many years. Her dad was... Well, not a good guy. So her parents divorced while she was young. Anyway, she came to me one day with this idea and a few months later she'd had her first fundraiser. The foundation has done wonders for her spirit and she's really been able to make a difference. At least most of the time she seems okay."

Toni sensed there was more to that statement. "What do you mean?"

"Oh, I shouldn't run my mouth."

"Well, when I left the other day, a really handsome man showed up. That has to make a woman's day."

Carol narrowed her eyes. "Was he tall, blond?"

Toni felt bad for pretending ignorance, but she nodded. "Yeah, I think so."

"That's probably her fiancé. I love Olivia, but she has always had bad taste in men. Something about that guy isn't right. For one, he popped the question to her after they'd only been together barely four months."

Toni's eyebrow shot up. While she never got to that point with Paul, she did remember that he moved fast. He claimed to be head over heels in love with her two years ago.

His type of love landed her in the hospital.

"Have you talked to Olivia about your feelings?"

Carol shook her head. "It wouldn't do any good. She loves him. And he can do no wrong in her eyes. Oh look, there comes my help. Thank God!"

Toni looked up to see who Carol was referring to. She wasn't sure if she dropped her mouth open, but she was definitely in shock.

Jade Lewis walked up to them and went straight towards the stroller. "Hey, babies." There was still some slight bruising to Jade's face, but she appeared to be in good working order.

Toni asked, "Is this your cousin?"

"Yes. Hey, Jade, meet my new client." Carol looked back at Toni with pleading eyes. "Well, at least I hope you'll be a new client after today."

Jade turned her attention in their direction. For a minute she didn't seem to recognize Toni, then her eyes changed as though she was afraid.

Carol chatted along not noticing her cousin's discomfort. "I'm so glad you are up and about, but I didn't expect you to disappear." Carol turned to

Toni. "Jade was in the bed most of last week. Somebody attacked her."

Jade moved around like she needed to go to the bathroom. "I'm all good now."

"Jade, I'm glad to see you're healing from your injuries," Toni said.

Carol looked between both women. "Do you two know each other?"

"We met last week," Toni explained, "any news from the police, Jade?"

Carol interrupted before Jade could speak, "No news at all. And it could have been any of us who were attacked."

"Sounds like someone was there to commit a robbery. I heard about it when I was meeting with Olivia," Toni added.

Carol nodded, "I don't know who had that kind of gumption, but they managed to steal an expensive painting. Poor Jade here forgot her phone in the office. I guess she just walked into the middle of the robbery."

Jade looked around as if she was ready to run. "People do crazy things." She stared at Toni as though she had something on her mind. "It's good to see you again. I appreciate your help. I forgot your name."

"Toni. Toni Reed."

"Right, you said nothing happened to the guy who attacked you."

Toni's face grew warm. She couldn't remember how much she'd shared with Jade. "Well, I was able to press charges and had a trial."

"No jail time?" Jade asked.

Toni shook her head, "No, but my circumstances were different. It sounds like this person committed a few crimes. I imagine when they're caught, there will be several charges filed."

Carol looked back and forth. "Wow, you two really got to know each other last week."

Jade grabbed the stroller. "Look, why don't I take your kids home so you two can talk?"

"Okay, Jade. I appreciate it."

She watched Jade push the stroller away. *She sure wanted to get away fast.* Toni felt bad for judging her. She remembered her own desire to want to hide from the public for awhile. Dealing with the assault and trying to get back to a normal life was a process.

She turned towards Carol, "You said Jade is your cousin?"

Carol nodded. "Yea, she's more like a younger sister. We grew up together. Her mom wasn't around much so my parents raised her. She's had some troubles over the years. I think she's finally coming around though. My husband agreed to let her move in with us last year while I was pregnant with Jenny. She's been a huge help to my family and business."

What kind of troubles?

Toni didn't feel like now was the time to pry. "So, she does help you manage the social media?"

"Well, yes. Without her, I wouldn't be able to take on multiple clients."

She wasn't sure why, but something occurred to Toni. "So if I was to work with you, how do we work out passwords? Security is kind of important to me."

"Oh, we would sign a contract and I keep a password manager that encrypts the passwords. So your information is safe with me."

Toni nodded. "That's good to know." Her phone rang. She peered at her phone. *Oh no! Why is he calling?* She decided it was best to let the call go voicemail.

She asked Carol, "So, when can we get started?"

"I will email you some paperwork and an invoice for this month."

Toni's phone rang again. She sighed. "Carol, it was good to meet you. I need to take this call."

"Sure, no problem. I'll be in touch soon."

Toni nodded as Carol walked away. She grabbed the phone to answer the call. "Cam?"

"Finally. We really need to talk, Toni."

Her stomach sank, "You sound like I'm in some kind of trouble."

"I hate to tell you this, but yeah, you might be."

What in the world did I do?

Chapter 14

Friday, June 16 at 2:20 pm

Cam wouldn't share a single word with her on the phone. She sped to the police station wondering why there was urgency in his voice. Her first thought was her surprise run-in with Jade. In one week, the sketch she did with Jade had disrupted Toni's life. While she was looking for her last week, Toni had no clue she was going to run in to Jade today.

She huffed as she sprinted towards Cam's office. When she rounded the corner, she saw Cam talking to Captain Lester Gilliam. She paused, not sure if she should approach. The captain was a good friend of her father's. She could've been paranoid, but she wondered if they were talking about her.

Cam saw her and gave her a head nod in the direction of his desk.

She walked over to his desk and sat. *What is going on?* It occurred to her she could have jeopardized her role at the department. All she did was sketch a composite.

Finally, Cam walked over. He grabbed a pen and a legal pad from his desk. "Let's talk in here."

She jumped up and followed him into an interrogation room. Now, she was totally freaked out. After she entered the room, she turned. "What's going on? I didn't do anything to be treated like some suspect. What exactly do you think I did?"

Cam looked at her. "I wanted you to hear this from me and not someone else. Sit please. It's better if we talk in here." He pulled the chair out from the table.

She pulled out the other chair and sat across from him. Toni watched as Cam fiddled with his tie as though it was choking him. "I'm going to get right to it. Have you had contact with Paul Lambert?"

Oh no! She swallowed. "Yes."

He narrowed his eyes. "You purposely reached out to him? Why?"

"No, no! I ran into him while I was at the Niles Foundation."

"You went back there after we talked?"

"It was for a legitimate reason. I brought a set of paintings to donate. I spoke to Olivia about doing an event around domestic violence. She loved the idea and liked my work. On the way out, Paul stepped off the elevator. I was as surprised to see him as he was to see me."

"Well, Paul is claiming you're harassing him. He's requested a restraining order against you."

Toni stared at Cam still trying to figure out how this happened. "What? Are you serious? You can't believe that I've been harassing Paul Lambert. Why would I do that? I have a restraining order against him. He assaulted me."

Cam stared at her for what seemed like a full minute. "He claimed you have been sending him messages over the past few weeks like you were baiting him to contact you."

"I haven't emailed, phoned or contacted Paul in two years."

"But you knew Olivia was his fiancée. You showed up at his fiancée's office twice."

Toni grimaced. "Are you trying to accuse me of

something, Cam? You're sounding like you don't believe me. You know me."

"Yes, I do. I know you won't leave well enough alone. Your whole family is that way. You are all born investigators and fixers."

Toni stood up. "Well it looks like you've made your mind up. There's nothing else I have to say."

Cam stood. "Calm down, Toni. I'm not accusing you of anything. I wanted to be sure you haven't gone too far. Sit, please. This is important."

Toni sat back down.

Cam coaxed. "Let me help you. Tell me everything and don't leave anything out. Please."

"Look, I admit the first time I visited the Niles Foundation was out of curiosity about what happened to Jade. That sketch bothered me, but I had no intentions of meeting Olivia. We met and talked. She invited me back. The second time I had an appointment. Olivia knew my name. I wasn't hiding who I was and she didn't seem to know my past history with Paul."

Toni thought about that for a moment. "Or, at least she pretended like she didn't know. I guess it was weird how Paul just showed up. His phone call afterwards was even weirder."

Cam stopped scribbling on his legal pad. "So he

reached out to you? He broke the no contact order? When and why didn't you report him?"

"I...I guess because I brought it on myself."

"Toni, he still violated the order. You should have reported it. What did he say to you? Did he threaten you?"

Toni nodded, "He assumed I was trying to ruin his life. He told me to leave him and Liv alone. Look you can check my phone records, my emails or whatever you need. I have not been harassing him. What proof does he have? Is he even on his meds? He could just be making this stuff up."

"It's possible. Believe me, we're looking into his claims. In the mean time, you should lay low and avoid all contact. Is there anything else I should know?"

Toni blew out a breath. "I don't know if it matters, but I saw Jade again today."

Cam stared, "Why did you see Jade?"

"I didn't seek her out."

Cam shook his head. "You just happened to run into her?"

"I met Carol Landers today to discuss managing my social media. I had no idea Jade was her cousin. I didn't ask for any of this."

"I know. I'm just concerned about you. You're

like a magnet for trouble lately. At some point, you got to stop."

"You just accused me of harassing the man who assaulted me." Toni held up her hands before Cam could protest. "I think I have had enough of all of this myself."

Cam sighed. "So Jade is Carol's cousin. Does she have access to accounts?"

Toni nodded. "Olivia mentioned she trusted Carol with her foundation and personal accounts. Just makes me wonder more about Jade. I'm sorry. I know we were talking about me stopping with my unofficial investigation, but the woman was acting strange."

Cam answered her, "You're wondering if Jade really went back for her phone?"

Toni sat back and crossed her arms. "You're suspicious about her now? Why?"

Cam looked troubled. "I'm supposed to be on the victim's side here. I spoke to Jade earlier this week. Just to check on her and update her on the case. Let's just say something was off. I'd rather not go into it now. I'm responsible for bringing you in on this case."

"Neither one of us could have known a sketch was going to send me down this path. I'm glad you know Jade does have access to passwords for the Niles Foundation social media. Who's to say she doesn't have access to other passwords?"

Cam frowned. "You think Jade let somebody into the gallery to steal?"

"Was it a real assault or just a diversion for someone to get in and out? You said nothing showed on the cameras. Someone messed with the cameras."

Cam rubbed his head. "This is all turning out to be really strange. Which makes me think you should be a lot more careful. With Paul thinking you're harassing him, we certainly don't need you getting more involved in this case."

"By the way, did Paul mention when I supposedly started harassing him?"

Cam looked at his pad and flipped a page. "He claimed it's been a few weeks. He did mention he didn't understand why the sudden harassment because you both had moved on."

Toni said, "So it could be someone else and he just accused me because we ran into each other. And of course, I just happened to show up from a meeting with his fiancée."

Cam nodded, "That's what I'm thinking."

"Good. For awhile there I thought you didn't believe me."

"I know what Paul put you through. I know you have moved on from him. My goal here was to let you know and to be sure I protected you."

"That's why I saw you talking to the captain. How much did you tell him? You know he's friends with my dad."

"I told Captain Gilliam just enough. I didn't mention the composite and how this all started. Just your assault a few years ago."

"Thanks. I hope you can at least find out who else was in the building that night since Paul does have an alibi."

"Me too. I'm hoping the missing painting will lead to answers. I would really prefer if you stayed as far away from the folks at the Niles Foundation as possible."

Toni sighed. "The sad thing is I sincerely believe in the foundation's mission and I like Olivia."

"I'm sure there are other opportunities out there. I would like to see these paintings one day. In the meantime, make sure your paperwork is renewed with the judge."

Toni rolled her eyes. "Don't worry. I will head that way after I leave here."

Chapter 15

Saturday, June 17 at 8:24 am

On Friday nights, Toni usually stayed up 'til the early morning hours working on a project. Tonight was no different. To occupy her mind, she sat at her kitchen table making bracelets. She placed three bracelets to the side for her mama and her sisters. By two o'clock, she was exhausted. Leaving her jewelry making tools on the table, she made her way into the bedroom. Toni knelt by her bed and prayed. *"Lord, I don't know what's happening. I can't wish the past few weeks away, but I want to move forward. I want to be completely healed from past and to have the life you want for me. In Jesus name. Amen."*

The next morning, Toni woke up around seven o'clock. With her mind on her family, she grabbed her phone and sent a group text to her siblings to see if they could meet at their parents' house. Within the hour, she'd received affirmative responses from Jo, Cori and Asia. It was rare for all of her siblings to be available, even on a Saturday morning.

With most of her family involved in law enforcement, one of them was always in the know. At the time of her assault, the detective on that case sent word back to her dad who was chief of police at the time. Her family was at the hospital as the paramedics pushed her in on a stretcher.

They all took turns sitting with her in the hospital and when she came home. It was during that time she began to appreciate her family more, especially their support.

She called her parent's home. Her mom would be in her garden at this time of morning. She hoped her mom would hear the phone. When she answered, Toni sighed with relief.

Her mama's voice was warm and soothing, "I wondered when you would call. Captain Gilliam called your dad last night."

Toni cringed. "I was afraid of that since they've been friends forever. I don't know what's going on, Mama. I barely slept last night."

"When I didn't hear from you, I prayed God

would grant you peace. I know how worried you can get. God sees all and knows all. I'm getting ready to fix a late breakfast. Your father stirred later than usual this morning."

"Good because I kind of invited everyone to the house."

Her mama replied, "Well, I better get started cooking since I'll have a crowd this morning."

By eleven o'clock, she and her siblings had assembled at her parent's home. Toni appreciated being surrounded by her family in her parent's kitchen. She gobbled the healthy helping of grits, eggs, bacon and a buttermilk biscuit. Her stomach was grateful since she'd managed to skip dinner.

Her mom had made a feast. Toni grabbed another buttermilk biscuit from the center of the table. Eating seconds wasn't her thing. She'd noticed her dad looking at her with concern.

He grinned, "Well, its good to see you with a hearty appetite. You cleaned that plate in record time."

Cori said across from her. "This was comfort food. I'm sure you needed this, sis."

She nodded as she chewed.

Her dad looked at Cori, "Son, let's let the ladies

have the kitchen. I have some things to run by you."

"Sure, Dad." He looked over at Toni.

She smiled at her brother, sensing he didn't want to leave her side. Despite being adults they still had that twin connection.

After her dad and brother left, her mom started clearing the dishes from the table.

"A restraining order? Huh." Asia frowned. "The lawyer in me thinks Mr. Lambert has something to hide. I'm wondering if his fiancée even knows he assaulted you."

Toni placed her fork on her plate. "I thought about that. Still, I don't see why he would go this far and say I'm harassing him. I never once contacted him."

Jo nodded in agreement. "He certainly doesn't have any proof that you've been harassing him. Sounds like Paul has another woman out there not happy with him."

Toni held her head. "Cam didn't supply details. I am curious who the real culprit may be."

"There are always other victims. I told you that during your trial. I wish someone else had stepped forward back then so Mr. Lambert could have actually had some real jail time," Asia offered.

Her mama grabbed more dirty dishes from the table. "I agree with Asia. His fiancée may not know he has this other side to him."

Toni shook her head. "I'm not so sure she doesn't know. When I spoke to Carol, her social media manager—"

Asia interrupted. "The woman you're trying to hire?"

Toni rolled her eyes. "Yes. She said that Olivia had a habit of choosing the wrong guys. I have a feeling that Carol didn't care for Paul."

Jo asked, "How did Olivia react to you?"

Toni shook her head. "Olivia was the one who reached out to me. She could have ignored me the first time we met. She invited me back to see my paintings even after I told her my name."

Asia tapped her fingernails on the table. "But you said the whole reason you went over there was because you had this suspicion that Olivia could have been protecting Paul. She was his alibi, right?"

Toni nodded. "Yeah, I actually went looking for Jade."

Jo added, "The victim? What did you want to find out about her?"

Toni threw up her hands. "It didn't seem

possible to me that she didn't know Paul. Granted the composite may not be him, but she described someone who looked awfully close. She claimed she never saw the guy in the sketch before. I mean wouldn't you be suspicious when you find out she works as a volunteer for Paul's fiancee?"

Mama sat and let out a breath like she was worn out. "Baby girl, I'm too tired from listening to all of this. I can understand why you've been bothered. We all felt like Paul got a slap on the wrist after the way he hurt you."

"I just wanted to be sure if he was involved with hurting another woman that he received justice." Toni held her head down. Her emotions were bubbling to the surface making her eyes water.

Jo leaned forward and touched her hand. "This is Cam's case. What did he say?"

Toni sniffled and wiped at her eyes before lifting her head. "Cam's first thought was this whole thing started from a robbery. That Jade was in the wrong place at the wrong time. I hope I'm not messing up his case, " she frowned, "but I think even he has doubts now."

Toni rubbed her head. "I'm so confused. I was minding my own business. My life was going well...at least I thought it was."

Asia crossed her arms. "I'm just happy you had sense enough to renew your no contact order. If you need legal counsel, I can arrange that. Hopefully, this whole thing with Paul will blow over because he should have never called you. You could press charges against him, you know?"

Toni gave her sister a look of panic. "No. I don't intend to get into it with Paul again. And I have no intentions of going back to see his fiancée. He made that pretty clear. In fact, the paintings can go back in the closet where they've been."

Mama shook her head. "Well, I hope you don't do that. Remember we talked about this the other day. Just pray on what you should do. It's obvious you've been led in a direction to help someone else who may be in the same place you once were."

"Yeah, Toni. There are women's shelters and other organizations you can reach out to who always need assistance," Jo added.

Toni stood and grabbed her bag from the side counter. "Well, you may be on to something." She took out the bracelets and handed one to her mama and each of her sisters. "I haven't shown you these bracelets yet. Have I?"

Asia took a bracelet and slid it on her wrist. "When did you start making these?"

"A few months ago. They're my new product line."

Asia admired the bracelet on her arm. "Girl, you run your own business. You can easily incorporate your artwork and use it for charities. I'm no tax lawyer, but I know people who can help you set up a nonprofit."

"That's a good idea. Why don't you spend some time establishing your own fundraiser?" Jo smiled.

Toni shrugged, "I guess it didn't occur to me that my art could be used for a bigger cause. It just all seems like a lot of work."

Mama interjected, "Maybe this is what you need to focus on, Toni. Let Cam do his job for that young woman. If Paul has done more harm, he will eventually receive what he has sown."

Toni sat back down. She'd asked God to help her move forward. Her family had encouraged her. She would put this all behind her and remain open to what God had planned for her.

Why do I still feel on edge?

Chapter 16

Wednesday, June 19 at 10:05 am

Toni was determined to refocus her efforts after talking with her family. She researched more about Domestic Violence Month and purchased various accessories including purple ribbon. She stayed up late several nights in a row trying out new bracelet designs.

This morning, she lingered in bed much later than usual. Her mind was filled with new ideas, really good ideas. She reached over to grab her moleskin notebook from her nightstand. The sun was high, so she didn't bother to turn on the lamp as she scribbled her thoughts.

She circled the last idea on her list. She needed to touch base with her friend who was a screen printer. Toni tapped the page with her pen as she mulled the idea over. She'd never experimented with fabric or cloth before. Nevertheless, she couldn't set aside the feeling that she could make even more of a contribution with a clothing line. Her paintings would be perfect.

The phone rang. She placed her notebook on the nightstand and reached for her phone.

Really? She's calling back now.

Toni had pretty much given up on Carol Landers. A week had passed with no contact from the woman. Probably for the best since Olivia recommended her.

Toni answered on the third ring. "Hello."

"Toni, how are you? This is Carol. Carol Landers."

She hoisted her legs over the edge of the bed. "I thought you forgot about me."

"Oh no! No, no. My little girl has been sick. We had to take her to the ER Saturday night. She was running a fever. Apparently, she caught some kind of virus. The doctors still aren't sure. She wasn't released until yesterday."

Toni sucked in a breath, "I'm sorry to hear that. I'm glad your daughter is doing better."

Carol's voice shook with emotion. "It's been an ordeal. I finished working on your work order agreement last Friday. I emailed it to you... or at least I thought I did. When I didn't hear from you, I looked at my email and there it was sitting in my draft folder. Silly me."

Toni stood. "It's okay. I assumed you changed your mind or something."

"What? No, why would I do that? I want to work with you. I've been admiring your work. You're very talented."

"Thank you." Toni swallowed. "In that case, you should know who I am and that working with me could be a problem."

"Oh?"

Toni sat on the edge of the bed. She took a deep breath. "Olivia may or may not know this by now, but I used to date Paul. At the end of our relationship, things got ugly. Basically, he assaulted me. I stayed in the hospital a few days. I pressed charges. We had a trial, he pretty much got a slap on the wrist with probation and a restraining order."

"Oh my! Toni, I don't think Liv knows any of this. She would've mentioned it to me. We've had lots of talks about Paul."

"Well, I ran into Paul while I was at Olivia's office. He contacted me afterwards and told me to stay away from her. I do intend to keep my distance, and I'm not quite sure about us working together. She's your friend so I wanted you to know the truth."

Carol had grown quiet.

Is she still there? "Carol?"

The woman made a sound like she was in pain. "Toni, you have to talk to Olivia."

Toni gripped her comforter. "Why? I can't do that. Did you hear anything I said?"

"Yes, I heard every word. And, you've confirmed my fears. I've felt like Paul wasn't the man for Liv. In fact, there has been a few times I've seen Liv with bruises."

"Bruises? You said you've seen this more than once?"

"Yes, the first time she claimed she tripped over her cat and I believed her. But the second time, was only a few weeks ago. She came to a meeting wearing shades. She claimed her eyes were sensitive to the light, but I saw the bruise when she turned her head. Toni, there was no way she fell. Someone hit her in the face."

Toni rubbed her head. "He's escalated. Or maybe he's been like this all the time." She thought out loud. "I wonder how many other women Paul has abused?"

"You've got to convince Liv to break up with him. She may listen to you."

Toni shook her head despite the fact Carol couldn't see her over the phone. "I don't think that's my place."

Carol pleaded with her, "Please reconsider."

Toni thought about something else. *Why was Olivia so friendly towards me? Did she know who I was the whole time and wanted to reach out to me?*

She let out a long sigh. "Carol, I'm not making any promises, but I'll see about talking to Liv."

"You could be saving her life."

"I need to ask you a question. It's off topic. Sort of."

"Okay."

"You were at the fundraiser that night Jade was attacked right?"

Carol responded, "Yes."

"So Detective Noble questioned you? Did he ever show you the composite?"

Carol sucked in a breath. "Yes, I was in Liv's office. He asked me if I recognized or had seen the man." The woman sniffed. "I thought he looked familiar."

"Like who?" Toni coaxed.

"He reminded me of Paul, but I didn't say that. Liv was standing right there. Besides, I saw him drive off with Liv in his car that night."

Toni thought out loud. "So his alibi is tight. They left before Jade was attacked. Since you were together, how did Liv react to the composite?"

"Liv looked at it for a long time, but she said she didn't know him. When the detective showed the sketch to me, I said the same even though I thought it looked like Paul."

Toni's head was spinning. She was right back where she'd desperately been trying to escape. "Who found Jade?"

"I did. She came with me. My mother-in-law was watching the kids that night, but I needed to get home. Those fundraisers can be so exhausting. She was taking so long to come back, I went inside to get her."

"You didn't pass anyone?"

"No, it was quiet. It took me a while to find Jade because I wasn't sure where she left her phone. I found her sitting on the floor outside the office where she was attacked. What are you thinking, Toni?"

Toni sighed. "Has Jade ever seen Paul before?"

"Yes, a few times. She knew who he was."

"Well, did she see Paul pick up Liv?"

Carol was quiet. "I believe so, yes. She went back upstairs after they'd left. Only Annie and the two of us remained. I talked with Annie until she went home. That's when I went looking for Jade."

Toni closed her eyes. She wondered who really attacked Jade and why the woman focused on Paul's face.

Was it just because she saw him or something else?

Chapter 17

Thursday, June 20 at 10:44 am

"Has this ever happened to you?"

Toni had called her mentor, Bobby Askins, for advice. He asked her to meet him at Joe's Coffee Shop where they'd met often after a session. It was no Starbucks, but it was a favorite among cops since the owner was a former cop.

Bobby was in his late sixties and since his hand had grown unsteady, he retired from the force over a year ago. His composites were legendary in the department, resulting in over one hundred arrests. He was a cop himself who did the composites as a part of his usual beat on the street.

He took a long swig of his coffee and nodded. His voice was deep and raspy from years of smoking. "You know, the human mind is a piece of work. I have had many people describe a face to me what they thought they'd seen. One woman kept focusing on how big this guy's eyes were. By the time I finished drawing the sketch, I felt like I'd drawn an alien."

Toni laughed. "Did they put that one out to the media?"

He shook his head. "No, but the funny thing was, the guy they caught did have big eyes. Not that big, but it made me think of what people focus on. I suspect with this woman, her mind may have focused on this guy Paul since she'd just seen him."

Toni added, "And she lives with Carol. She could have overheard Carol mention Liv's bruises."

Bobby nodded. "So Jade heard about the abuse and her brain wired what she thought she saw."

"I guess. It's always bothered me how Jade could see anything. There was some light, but she was so detailed. In theory, if the person knew she'd fully seen his face, why let her live?"

Bobby coughed, "It was a robbery. Maybe they wanted to keep her quiet, you know, just scare her until they could make their getaway."

"The painting hasn't shown up yet. It was worth a lot of money."

"You know, Toni. We just sketch what the victim or witness shares with us."

Toni rubbed her temples. "But we want to make sure the composite helps the police find the perp."

"You got to stop beating yourself up, kid. You did your part."

She grabbed her coffee cup and sipped. Bobby was right. She did all she could do for Jade.

But what about Olivia?

She'd told Carol she would think about it. Did she even have an option? This case started with Jade, but somehow Toni had been pulled in for reasons she could never have imagined.

Toni sensed a shadow over her. She looked up to see Cam standing at the table.

He reached out to shake Bobby's hand. "Good to see you, Bobby."

"You too. Guess I can't call you Rookie anymore."

Cam flashed a smile, "I hope I've grown in this job some." He turned to Toni. "I've been looking for you."

Bobby held up his cup. "Here, take my seat. I need a refill and I see some buddies who just walked in." With some effort, Bobby pulled his massive body from the booth. He placed his hand on Toni's shoulders. "Proud of you, kid. You're doing good. Don't let the strange ones get to you."

Cam sat across from her. Toni didn't look at him right away. She sipped her coffee. She'd been talking so much to Bobby, she'd barely drunk a third of the coffee.

"How are you, Toni?"

She eyed Cam. Despite the concern she saw in his brown eyes, she raised her eyebrow. "You mean am I staying out of trouble?"

"Don't put words in my mouth."

She twisted her lips. "Sorry. I've been a bit on edge lately."

Cam shrugged. "It's okay. You've been following your gut. That's what a good detective does."

"I'm not a detective." She cocked her head, "What's going on? You said you've been looking for me."

"Let's just say you don't have to worry about the restraining order or Paul Lambert anymore."

"No?"

"Paul was definitely being harassed and we're tracking down that person as I speak."

Toni raised her eyebrow. "You're not going to give any details."

He shook his head. "I think it's for the best if I

didn't. Besides, you looked pretty intense talking to Bobby."

Toni crossed her arms, her mind on Olivia. "I should let you know I talked to Carol Landers again. You remember her?"

Cam thought for a second. "I had a chance to interview her after Jade's assault. Ms. Landers found Jade. Why are you two still talking?"

"Legit reason. Remember I was thinking about hiring her as my social media manager? Anyway, I decided to be honest with her about my history with Paul. She shared some interesting things with me about Olivia."

"Like what?"

"Paul could be abusing Olivia."

Cam sighed. "Well, guys like that tend to treat women the same. He may have a mental illness, but he's also arrogant and grew up in a wealthy family. He's used to getting what he wants. I imagine he probably hurt someone before you. You know there's nothing law enforcement can do unless the victim press charges."

"I'm well aware of the process. Remember, I pressed charges, went to trial and everything." Toni tapped her fingernails on the table. "Asia mentioned it would have been good for my case if other women had come forward."

Cam nodded, "Yeah. I agree. So now that you have this information about Olivia, you're still keeping your distance right?"

Toni looked at Cam. "Carol thought I should talk to her."

Cam shook his head, "No."

"What if something happens to her? You know, I was curious why she was so interested in my paintings. Now—"

"You're feeling obligated to help her?"

Toni shook her head. "It's more than that. It's like every since I did that composite, I've been led down this path that leads to Paul Lambert. I'm thinking he was involved with assaulting one woman, but he's really hurting a woman who's planning to marry him."

Cam leaned forward. "I can't sit here and pretend like I know what you're feeling. I don't like what that guy did to you. A man should never put his hands on a woman, but I don't want you getting in his way again."

"I don't plan to. Anyway, have you gotten anywhere with Jade's case?"

"No. There hasn't been any other leads. Our

tech guys are looking into the security company that runs the cameras."

Toni's phone rang. She peered at the screen.

Cam asked, "Did you want to answer that call?"

She shook her head. "I don't recognize the phone number." She declined the call and pushed her phone to the side.

"Well, you should know I was talking to Bobby here because the composite is still bothering me. Something happened to Jade. But, I don't think Jade really saw her attacker."

Cam rubbed his lips together. "I know."

Toni frowned, "You do?"

"I've looked at that sketch over and over again. You're right. It looks like Paul. I even double-checked Paul's alibi based on your being bothered by it."

Toni looked at him. "I'm sure she was just traumatized and described what her memory gave her. According to Carol, Paul had just left with Olivia. It's possible that Jade overhead Carol telling Olivia she needed to cut things off with Paul."

"I get it. Still, it doesn't help me track down a $10,000 painting and find out who was in that area that night. I'm literally in the dark."

Her phone rang again. Toni studied the display. "It's the same phone number."

Cam asked, "Is it a local number?"

"Yes."

"Well, maybe just answer it. The worse it could be is a telemarketer, right?"

Toni touched the accept button on her phone. "Hello?"

"Toni, thank goodness. I wanted to be sure to get you on the phone as soon as possible."

Unbelievable. Toni peered over at Cam before turning her attention back to the caller. "Is this Olivia?"

"Yes, I'm so sorry for not saying who I was. I was just waiting to hear back from you. I've been thinking a lot about your suggestions for an event in October. I would love to run some ideas by you."

Toni shook her head. She glanced up to see Cam mouthing, "What is this about?"

She waved at him. "That sounds great, Olivia. Sure, when do you want to meet?"

"How about tomorrow afternoon around four o'clock? I know it's a Friday, but I wanted to make sure you had the weekend to think over the ideas."

"Okay, I can make that work."

"Great! I'll see you tomorrow, Toni."

"Bye, Olivia."

Before she hung up the call, Cam was already asking, "What are you doing?"

Toni rubbed her head. She wondered the same thing. "I went to Olivia about doing an event in October that... centered around Domestic Violence Month."

"What? Cam exclaimed. "That's the craziest thing I've ever heard. I mean not the fact that you're doing an event. That's admirable." Cam shook his head, "Who you're planning the event with... Is this not the same woman who you just said might be being abused?"

Toni nodded. "I'm just as lost as you are. I've been lost the entire last few weeks. The only conclusion I can come to is there is a woman reaching out for my help, as weird as it may seem."

"That's what you think is going on?"

Toni shrugged. "What are you thinking?"

He nodded. "I don't know what to think. Look, just do me one favor. Don't stop listening to your instincts. What time are you meeting her tomorrow?"

"Four o'clock at her office."

"Alright," Cam placed both palms on the table and leaned forward slightly, looking intensely at

Toni. "I have to go. Please stay in touch. Tell your folks where you are tomorrow too. Just don't take any chances."

"You seem to be looking at this case a lot differently now. I hope I haven't interfered that much to make you second guess anything."

Cam stood, "Toni, I know it seemed like I wasn't listening to you. I heard your concerns and yes, I totally agree something hasn't been right about this entire case." He put his hand on her shoulder. "Watch your back."

She placed her hand on his and nodded. "I will."

As she watched Cam walk away, his words kept looping in her mind.

Watch your back. Watch your back.

Chapter 18

Thursday, June 29 at 10:37 pm

"Pray."

Toni had called her mother before going to bed.

Her mother asked, "This woman has never brought up your past with Paul?"

"No," Toni said. "I know she has to know by now."

"Well, have you thought that may be something has changed? She may have seen the light and let Paul go."

"You know that thought occurred to me too. Either way, before we talk about anything, I need her to know what Paul did and that he's the reason for those paintings."

"I agree with you. Make sure she understands the conflict of interest here, especially if she's still involved with Paul. You already said God has given you ideas to pursue. You can hear her out, but you have other options."

"You're right."

Her mother yawned. "Be sure you do what I just said."

Toni grinned, "I will. Good night, Mama."

Toni smiled and hung up the phone. She slipped to her knees.

Dear Lord, I don't know what I'm walking into tomorrow. You know my feelings these past few weeks have been conflicted. I never thought I had to see or talk about Paul Lambert again. Here he is in my life again along with other women. One woman seems really troubled and found herself fixated on Paul's face and another woman who seems okay with marrying him despite the fact he's mistreating her. God grant protection for me and prayerfully guide me according to your will in this situation. In Jesus name, I pray. Amen.

Friday, June 21 at 3:54 pm

Toni woke the next morning grateful for a restful night. As the day continued, her mind raced and her stomach grumbled. By three o'clock, she left her apartment to head down I-77. When she finally arrived, she sat in the car for a few minutes. Remembering what Cam said yesterday, she texted.

Just letting you know I'm here.

She waved at the security guard as she passed. When the elevator arrived, she waited as people piled out. Toni noted the evident excitement for the weekend on most of the faces that passed her. She chuckled to herself as she entered the elevator. *Definitely a Friday afternoon,* she thought. While the elevator rose to the third floor, she couldn't identify the emotions twisting inside of her. She simply didn't know what to expect in the next few moments when she met with Olivia Niles.

Could be our last meeting ever.

When the elevator doors opened, she was surprised Annie wasn't at the desk. Toni stepped off the elevator, not really sure what to do. She checked her phone. It was almost four o'clock. She stepped into the waiting room area and sat. If no one approached in the next five minutes, that was reason enough for her to leave.

The offices were relatively quiet before, but it seemed too quiet to her. She peered around waiting for someone to walk by.

She fiddled with her phone for a while and noticed Cam hadn't texted her back. Cam, her mom, Jo and Cori knew she was here. She'd used some sense today.

Suddenly, she'd heard voices in the back. That was the first time she'd heard any sign of life in five minutes. It sounded like someone had just opened an office door. Toni sat still to see who was coming.

She froze as she watched Olivia being escorted into the lobby by none other than Paul Lambert. Paul exclaimed, "Oh, good. She's here. Why don't we have proper introductions now?"

Toni jumped up. "What is this?"

"Oh, no. Toni, I'm sorry. Paul wasn't supposed to be here."

Paul stepped forward. "But how convenient for you to be here, Toni. I was sorry about what I did to you. I was a bad boy for not taking my meds, okay? But that doesn't give you the right to come back into my life."

Toni's body felt like an electrical current was running through it. "I haven't been in your life for two years. Nor do I care anything about you now."

Paul stared back and forth between them. "Right. I should've known something was up when I saw you the other day." He looked at Olivia. "We were happy. You can't break things off with me."

They broke up. That's good. Now I need to get out of here.

Toni looked towards the elevator wishing she'd listened to Cam.

"You're not thinking about leaving now are you?" Paul spat. "The party is just getting started."

"Party? Look, I came here because Olivia showed some interest in *my* work. I'm more than happy to take my paintings elsewhere. If you messed up with her, nobody is to blame but you."

Olivia shook her head. She turned to Paul. "You need to go. It's over." She yanked her arm away from Paul and ran over to the desk, "I'm calling security."

"What security?" Paul yelled, pointing at Toni. "You invited this woman into our lives. And, for what?" He reached over and grabbed Olivia.

Oh no!

Toni couldn't stand by and watch this. She looked over at the table and grabbed the lamp, yanking it out of the wall. "Let her go."

Paul stopped and looked at her. "Or what? You're going to bludgeon me with the lamp. Take your best shot, Toni."

Before Toni took a step, a sound exploded in her ear. She gasped as something whizzed past her ears.

The next few seconds felt like minutes as she watched in horror as something slammed into Paul's chest, causing an explosion of blood on his shirt.

Toni observed the shock on Olivia's face as the blood spattered.

She registered Paul's eyes as he stared past her before he crumbled to the ground.

Toni looked at the elevators. The doors never opened.

She turned around slowly not knowing who was behind her.

Toni stepped back like she'd been slapped. "Annie?"

Annie stood with her feet apart, hair disheveled with the gun still in her hand. "He had it coming!"

Behind her Olivia shrieked. "Oh no! What did you do?"

Toni turned around to see Olivia on the floor cradling Paul's head. She looked up. "Help him. Don't let him die like this."

Toni reached for her phone.

"Don't!" Annie screamed. She pointed the gun towards Toni. "He deserves to die."

Toni stepped back. Her mind whirled despite the panic creeping from her head to her toes.

Troubled Heart

I've been looking at the wrong woman the whole time.

She hoped Cam picked up on something she never saw coming.

Chapter 19

Friday, June 21 at 4:33 pm

Toni took a breath. She spoke low. Her voice steadier than she felt, "You set this all up. Why?"

Annie looked wild-eyed, like she'd been taking something. "I thought it was past time we all had a group meeting. You and Liv have just been ripping around each other and no one was dealing with the elephant in the room. I just couldn't stand it anymore."

Toni turned from Olivia back to Annie. "Annie, we're not your enemy here. Put the gun down. You shot who you wanted. It doesn't need to end like this. Why are you doing this to yourself? He could die."

Annie bit her lip, but she didn't lower the gun.

Toni continued. She had to know the truth now.

"How long have you known Paul? It seems like you've been waiting for this opportunity."

Annie smiled. "The picture grew bigger the day you walked in here. Despite Jade's crazed mind, you sketched him perfectly."

Toni gasped. Jade had manipulated her the entire time she was sketching. "I don't understand. What's your involvement here?"

Annie's smile quivered. "I know you tried, Toni. I was in the courtroom when they had him on trial. I tried to talk to your lawyer and tell him about Amber."

Toni shook her head. "Who's Amber?"

"My sister. She wasn't strong like you. After what Paul did to her in high school, she was never the same. She finally killed herself six years ago. I told your lawyers. Then, I saw how he just got a slap on the wrist again. I felt bad for you. I wanted to do something, but what could I do?"

"Then I came to work for Liv here. I loved working here until the day she introduced me to her fiancée. The same man responsible for killing my sister."

Olivia's face crumpled, "You said she killed herself."

Annie yelled, shaking the gun towards Olivia.

"After he raped her! He never paid for what he did. She suffered. My parents sent her to a psychiatric ward because she couldn't cope. And I watched him go on with his life. That miserable creep!"

Toni clasped her hands together. *Father God, protect us.*

"You know what, Toni." Annie continued. "He really didn't get rehabilitated. Poor Jade. Jade fell in love with him. They were in the same rehabilitation place. He used her and threw her out like trash when he was finished with his little sentence."

Toni was confused. "Jade? Jade knew Paul? And you... you helped Jade with the robbery?"

Annie narrowed her eyes. "That was all Jade and her friends. She'd been snooping around here. Carol trusted her with everything. I haven't figured out how someone like her got access to the security though."

Annie shrugged. "But Jade did do something right for a change, even if her plan was a bit misguided."

Toni shook her head. "She described Paul's face."

Paul was looking so close to death right now, Toni wasn't sure he could be saved. The guy did some horrible things, but this was not the way to handle it. He needed to be behind bars to think long and hard about his ways.

Annie twirled the gun. "And she wanted to get back at Olivia. That girl thought Paul was supposed to be hers. At first, I was angry because she really wanted to hurt Olivia so much that her pea brain couldn't remember Paul had left with Olivia." Annie smiled. "But it worked out better than I could've planned. When you said your name, I knew who you were and I knew why you were really here."

Toni narrowed her eyes. "No you didn't."

"You were looking for Jade. Which means you wanted to know who really attacked her. You wanted to find out if it was really Paul," Annie said.

Toni took a deep breath, "And you've been the person harassing him. You've been after him all this time to get vengeance on your sister. It wasn't a mere coincidence when he showed up the other day when I was leaving. Just like today. You saw I was coming to see Olivia and you wanted a confrontation."

"I know this man. You have to bait him for the real Paul Lambert to show up. Just in time too, since Liv here came to her senses and finally gave Paul his ring back."

Toni and Liv stared at each other. They'd both been played.

Or had they?

Toni didn't have time to complete the thought. The lights blinked. Annie and Olivia both screamed. Toni dropped to ground.

The lights flickered again and she heard, "Put your hands in the air."

Toni pressed her hands to her head as a spray of gunshots rang out.

God, let this be over soon.

Chapter 20

Friday, June 21 at 5:31 pm

Toni sat crouched for what seemed like forever. She thought she heard her name, but she was unwilling to move.

"Toni. It's me, Cam. You're okay."

She peered up. "Oh my God. I should've listened to you."

"You're alright, now. God was looking out. I got your text. It came just as we were cracking open some other things. Look, let me get you out of this location."

"What happened to Annie?"

Cam held her gaze and shook his head. "You don't want to see. She didn't make it."

"But..."

"She had a firearm, Toni. Nothing good comes from that. Let's get you out of here."

Toni looked to see paramedics arriving in the elevator.

Cam encouraged her inside.

"Is that for Paul?"

Cam sighed. "He's still breathing. Barely."

Toni nodded. When the elevator stopped, Cam walked her to a room behind the security desk.

The white haired guard stood at the door.

Cam said, "Take care of these ladies."

"Yes, sir. Ma'am, come in here. Can I get you some coffee?"

Toni shook her head. She looked over and found Olivia crumbled in the corner, twisting her fingers. Her face was wet with mascara streaks. Toni noticed the blood spatter on Olivia's pink blouse.

Not knowing what else to do, Toni sat beside her. "It'll be okay."

Olivia trembled. "I can't believe any of this. They won't tell me anything about Paul or Annie. I wanted to go with him. There was so much blood. Do you think he's going to make it?"

"I don't know," Toni swallowed, "Olivia, did you know who I was all this time?"

Olivia shrank back like she was afraid of getting

hit. "Not at first. I wasn't a part of any of this, if that's what you're thinking." She hung her head low. "My mother would be ashamed if she knew I was with Paul. When I started thinking about what my mother would say if she were here, I knew I couldn't marry Paul. He was nice one minute, and then he—"

"Would turn on you the next. Did you know he was bipolar?"

Olivia shook her head. "Your name was familiar to me. It wasn't until I looked up your name that I saw the articles about the trial. I started trying to get a grip on Paul's behavior and I looked for his pills."

Toni nodded, "I'm glad you found out about him before you walked down the aisle."

Olivia shuddered. "My dad had issues. I didn't understand why my mom left him when I was a little girl. But later, when I was in college, she explained how my dad's behavior was too much."

Toni patted Olivia's hand. "Believe me. You don't know someone until they show their true selves. Paul was good at hiding."

Olivia asked, "Did you know who I was? Were you here to help?"

Toni laughed. "I knew you were Paul's fiancée,

but I honestly didn't know what in the world I thought I was doing. I have lived my last two years in recovery mode."

They sat in silence.

Olivia asked, "I still don't want him to die."

"I don't either, but I also don't want Annie, Jade, you, me or anyone else to have to experience someone going free for doing us harm."

"Poor Annie," Olivia whimpered. "I always thought she was a little bit overprotective."

Toni gave her a side eye, "Girl, you think? She was packin'. Can you say Annie Oakley?"

They snickered quietly as Toni's joke fell flat.

She was grateful to see Cam peek in. "How are you two holding up?"

Olivia didn't respond.

Cam made eye contact with Toni before stepping aside to let a female detective enter the room. The woman spoke to Olivia, "Ms. Niles, I'm Detective Gwen Matthews. Are you ready to let me take your statement, Ma'am?"

Olivia nodded.

Cam looked at Toni. "Detective Matthews will want a statement from you too. I asked her to give you some time. I can call someone to take you home. It might not be a good idea for you to drive right now."

Toni stood and waved her hand back and forth in the air as if she were erasing his suggestion. "I'm fine. I can talk to her. Tell me what you know."

Cam sighed. "This is not the time."

"Yes, it is. Annie set this whole thing up, all to get back at Paul. You got to admire her tenaciousness on seeking revenge for her sister."

Cam cleared his throat. "You're right. She's been slowly going after him."

"I walked right into her plan."

"Let's sit. I'll tell you what I have pieced together."

Toni sat. "Start with the robbery because that still doesn't make sense."

Cam sat beside her and rubbed his hands together. "The robbery was Jade and her friends. She's been under the influence of a group of friends for a long time. She let them know about what the gallery had and they set up a plan. One of her friends had a brother who worked at the security company. That's how I was able to start connecting dots. I think the only reason why Jade was supposedly assaulted was to prevent her cousin from catching her in the act."

Toni frowned. "She was probably also setting up a decoy for her friends to conveniently get away with the painting."

"That would be correct. The good news is we brought Jade in a while ago and asked her to give us the whereabouts of her friends. So we expect to pick them up along with the painting soon. I don't know what they were thinking. There was no way they could sell that painting. It was a one of a kind."

Toni said. "I think it was more about Jade trying to hurt Olivia. From what Annie said, Jade was in love with Paul. Speaking of Annie, what's her story?"

"Remember when were talking about your case and how it would've been nice if other women came forward."

"Yes. You looked up other women?"

Cam nodded. "I did. The crazy thing is there were quite a few cases before you. I think your lawyer reached out to them, but they just didn't want to come forward."

"Annie said she did."

Cam nodded. "She did. Your lawyer, for whatever reason, chose not to bring her forward."

Toni frowned. "Why?"

"Possibly because Annie was convinced Paul killed her sister."

"She committed suicide." Toni sighed. "Still, her voice probably should've been heard. Maybe Paul would have served some real jail time. And none of this would have happened. I mean look at Jade. She met Paul in rehab."

"Wow, you know about that too."

Toni narrowed her eyes. "When did you find out?"

"When I talked to Carol again. She mentioned Jade had spent time in rehab and that she had a hard time getting her husband to let Jade stay with them."

"I bet. So you've been working out all these leads. How did you know to come here with backup?"

"My gut."

"Really?"

"I told you yesterday I didn't have a good feeling about you meeting with Ms. Niles, especially after the run-in with Paul. Her phone call was just a little too..."

"Suspicious. You think she had any ideas about any of this?"

"No. I think you both were pawns in some other

women's quests for justice. It just happened that your quest was good and I believe there was a higher purpose."

"Letting that Reed trait take over wasn't a bad thing."

"I like that about your family. I especially like it in you. So why don't we get your statement so we can get you home?"

Toni nodded. She hooked her arm inside Cam's and allowed him to lead the way.

Epilogue

Three months later, October

Toni took a breath before stepping into the gallery. She'd left the stage about thirty minutes ago where she delivered a passionate speech on domestic violence. Her voice was full of emotion from the past few years and recent months, but somehow she'd managed to get through it. The Reed family was all there lending their support, including her half-brother, Jax, who drove up from Atlanta.

She smiled and greeted people as they walked up to her. This was all still surreal to her to see her paintings framed on a gallery wall. After all that happened, it was indeed a God thing.

She looked across the room and saw Olivia walking towards her. In the past few months, the two women had become friends. They had experienced more together in a few months than many people experienced in a lifetime.

Olivia reached Toni and embraced her. She looked different from the last time Toni saw her a few weeks ago. She'd cut her long black hair and opted for a more stylish cut with bangs that hung to the side.

Toni grinned, "I love the new cut. It suits you."

Olivia clasped her hands together. "Thank you. I've been dreading doing it. But, it felt like I needed something new, especially with your event approaching. I really loved your speech. It was…"

Toni reached for Olivia's hand. "…what needed to be said. I couldn't have done this without you. I appreciate you pulling all this together in such a short amount of time especially after…" Toni's voice trailed off. She gently squeezed Olivia's hand and said, "You're braver than you think."

Olivia nodded. "I visited Paul's grave yesterday. I just felt like I needed to say some things even though he couldn't hear me."

"Sometimes you need to speak what's on your heart. God heard you."

Toni caught Cam looking at her from across the

room. She wanted to go over to him, but could tell Olivia had more to say.

Her and Cam had been trying out the dating thing for a few weeks now. He was her date tonight for the fundraiser. Ever since the incident, he'd been by her side.

Toni let go of Olivia's hand, folding her arms across her waist. "Have you talked to Carol? I heard that Jade has a trial date now."

Olivia shook her head. "Not yet."

"Do you really believe she didn't know the whole time what her cousin was up to?"

Olivia looked at her. "In my heart, I know Carol is a good person. I honestly don't think she knew about Jade. She loved her cousin and just wanted to help her. Maybe one day I'll talk to her." She turned her head away from Toni's gaze. "Just hard to trust anyone right now."

"I get it. You'll be happy to know I've been working with a therapist. I wanted to be sure I removed any old baggage."

Olivia clasped her hands. "Good for you! By the way, I see your boyfriend giving us the eye, so I'm going to get out of his way. Thanks again for everything, Toni."

Toni hugged Olivia, her mind still on that word.

Boyfriend.

She liked how that sounded.

Cam glided over. "Finally, I get you to myself."

She grinned. "We're surrounded by people."

"I only have eyes for you. Your speech was breathtaking, by the way. I saw a few folks blotting their eyes. I had to find something to stop the water leakage going on in my own eyes."

"Oh, Cam. I couldn't have done any of this without you. When I think about that day and Annie... I don't know."

"You're a smart woman, Toni. You knew something wasn't right and you were persistent. I'm proud of you."

She raised her eyebrow. "Are you sure? I mean I was sticking my nose in places I shouldn't have. My mama says that inquisitive nature is a Reed thing. But, it's also a gift."

Cam laughed, "I totally agree. You'd make a great detective."

"Nah. I'll leave the detective work to my boyfriend."

"Mmm, I liked the sound of that. Maybe in the future we can adjust that title a bit to something more permanent sounding."

"I like the sound of that, Mr. Noble."

Cam bent down. Despite being in the middle of a crowd of people, Toni had no trouble accepting his kiss.

About the Author

Tyora Moody is the author Soul-Searching Suspense books which include the Reed Family Novellas, Eugeena Patterson Mysteries, Serena Manchester Series, and the Victory Gospel Series. She is also the author of the nonfiction book, *The Literary Entrepreneur's Toolkit*, and the compilation editor for the Stepping Into Victory Compilations under her company, Tymm Publishing LLC.

As a literary-focused entrepreneur, she has assisted countless authors with developing an online presence via her design and marketing company, Tywebbin Creations LLC. Popular services include virtual event planning, book covers and book trailers.

To contact Tyora about book club discussions or for book marketing workshops, visit her online at TyoraMoody.com.

Books By Tyora Moody

REED FAMILY SERIES
Broken Heart, Book 1

EUGEENA PATTERSON MYSTERIES
Oven Baked Secrets, Book 2
Deep Fried Trouble, Book 1
Shattered Dreams: A Short Story

SERENA MANCHESTER SERIES
Hostile Eyewitness, Book 1

VICTORY GOSPEL SERIES
When Perfection Fails, Book 3
When Memories Fade, Book 2
When Rain Falls, Book 1

CPSIA information can be obtained
at www.ICGtesting.com
Printed in the USA
LVOW12s2128260317
528550LV00001B/18/P